BRUTAL RUIN

REVERSE HAREM MAFIA ROMANCE

BEAUTY & THE BRATVA

MIKA LANE

HEADLANDS PUBLISHING

BE THE FIRST TO KNOW...

Want more heat, heart,
and bad boys who know what they're doing?
Join my list and I'll send the steam straight to your inbox,
starting with a deliciously naughty story:

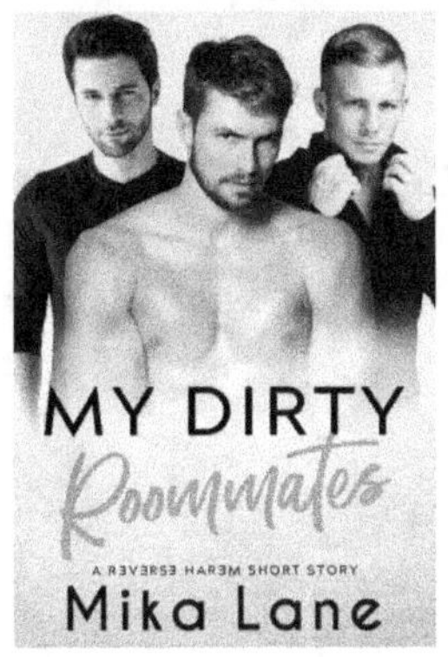

CHAPTER ONE

CHARLEIGH

"Stop. Here. Now."

I throw a crisp hundred at the cab driver. Without a word of thanks for his kindness, aside from my generous tip, I bolt from his car.

This is not the time for courtesies. Or manners. Thank-you's and polite smiles will have to wait for another day.

My head down, like that will keep anyone from staring at me and my strange appearance, I run into the Target store clear across town from where I began my journey, where the cabbie picked me up without question, gave me a ratty hoodie and base-ball cap to use as a disguise, and broke every speed limit on the way.

God bless him.

The drive was hellishly long for one that was only fifteen-minutes, no doubt the longest quarter hour I've ever lived. I suppose that's to be expected when you're running for your life.

I pull my cap low and tighten the drawstring on the hoodie. I'm covered from the waist up, which is a plus, but the bottom half of my body remains on full display. As I dash for the store, my slinky evening gown whipping around my legs, I stumble while I try to run in a pair of sky-high stilettos. I force myself to slow before I trip and fall, or worse, break an ankle. I don't need any more problems than I already have at the moment.

I know I look like a total freak, but a few minutes and a couple dollars spent at Target will fix all that. Target's good that way. A pair of jeans, a sweatshirt, sneakers, and a face scrubbed clean of all the makeup I'm wearing, and no one will know I was up for auction just an hour ago—an auction to sell my virginity.

That's right. Some sick fuck was going to pay a shit ton of money to pop my cherry. In fact, multiple men were going to fight over me with their checkbooks, bidding my price higher and higher, the winner determined by whomever had the deepest pockets.

Disgusting bastards.

But more than anything, right now, I need to keep a low profile. I'm hoping there won't be many people shopping since it's already ten p.m. With my eyes on the floor in front of me, I bolt straight for women's clothing. I don't want to catch anyone's eye. Or anyone's attention.

I know Target. This is my store. I'm momentarily comforted being here, at least as comfortable as anyone can be, scared to death and certain that bad men—very bad men—are right on my heels.

I'm pretty sure it's not natural, finding comfort when you know killers are after you, coupled with an awareness that your life could end at any moment when you're doing something as simple as walking through a store.

But what is normal about my life anymore?

I need the momentary relief from the adrenaline flooding every nook and cranny of my body, making my heart pound, my head ache, and my stomach churn from its force.

The irony. Adrenaline gives us the power to run away from dangerous situations. But it can also kill us.

If the bastards chasing me don't get to me first.

For years I have come to this very Target store to leisurely browse panties and socks, T-shirts and shorts, among other things. Those days are behind me now, I'm afraid, the ones consisting of the simple pleasure of walking around filling up my cart with all sorts of stuff I didn't know I needed. The curse—and hilarious meme—of the Target shopper.

But I'm a different person now, living a different life, and I scan in every direction to see if anyone has noticed my strange appearance—a fully made-up girl in a gold lamé evening dress wearing a baseball cap and tattered hoodie. If anyone ever looked like a weirdo trying to pull something off, it's me at this moment.

I push into the maze of clothing racks and breathe easier at my temporary sense of safety, a brief respite from the terror coursing through my veins. I'd like to stay here forever, in the cozy womb of Target clothing.

Squeezing between racks of dresses, overly packed with merchandise too close together to comfortably walk between, I've found the hiding place of my dreams. Surrounded, I'm barely visible, relieved no one's paying any attention to me. If I did catch a curious eye on the way in, they lost interest fast.

Just another weirdo passing through Target. Yup, that's me.

Thank you, universe, for this most miniscule of breaks.

After I catch my breath, I grab a pair of jeans, a T-shirt, and a light sweater and make a dash for the dressing room. I pull on my new things, stuff the cash hidden in my high-heels into my front pocket, and roll my dress, stilettos, and baseball cap into a ball, wrapping everything tightly in my hoodie. On the way out, I stuff my bundle into the bottom of a deep bin of clothing waiting to be returned to the racks by some unfortunate employee. By the time these items are found, I'll be long gone.

Now barefoot, I find a pair of sneakers to slip into, and in the fastest shopping trip ever, I snag a hat, underwear, sweats, a burner phone, and a back-pack. I take my haul to the register, where the nice cashier helps cut the tags off the things I'm wearing.

"Honey, where are the clothes you came in with?" she asks, looking me up and down.

"Tossed them. Didn't like them."

She looks at me for a moment and decides to say nothing.

In the store's Starbucks café, I settle into a corner table behind a column. I'm well-hidden, maybe even better than I was between the clothing racks, and it feels good. Tucking my hair down the back of my new sweater, I pull on my hat and load my backpack with my new purchases. I tear open my burner phone—the clerk in electronics corrected me, saying it was a 'prepaid phone'—insert the SIM card, and plug it into the charging outlet next to my table. While I'm waiting for the phone to juice up, I grab a coffee and a scone as the baristas are cleaning up for the day. My head pounds and I can't remember the last time I ate. I just know I couldn't keep anything down today, I was such a mess over the auction.

The auction I just ran away from.

I'm not sure whether or not I'm happy I escaped, because the words *what have I done?* are flitting through my thoughts like a flashing neon sign. Have I made my situation better? Or worse? The not knowing part is terrifying.

God help me.

While watching my new phone charge to fifteen percent and then twenty, I sip coffee and realize I'm not even sure who to call it with. This is the worst-planned escape in the history of lame-ass escapes. Actually, it wasn't planned at all. I saw an opportunity and took it. And to make my anxiety worse, it's ten-thirty p.m., and Target closes at eleven. It's only a matter of minutes before they start their friendly 'we're closing soon, please pay for your purchases' announcement.

I'm racing through my options. Or rather, lack of options. I can't spend the night here. They'd ferret me out for sure. These places have crazy robust security.

While I have no idea what my next steps are, I don't regret running. At least I don't think I do. I never would have forgiven myself if I hadn't tried to get out, to escape the Alekseevs holding me hostage. When the horrible Dimitri created a ruckus in the back of the room just before the auction, I saw an opportunity and grabbed it. Plain and simple. There were no thoughts running through my head other than *get to the door NOW*. Nothing about what I would do once I got there, where I'd go, or what would follow next.

But I got out, right? Isn't that the important thing?

I just need to figure out what to do now.

How lucky am I there was a cab letting out passengers right in front of the club? That the understanding driver sped off onto the freeway, no questions asked, and that he even gave me a hat and hoodie to wear?

How lucky am I that I'd thought to stuff a few hundreds into my shoe when dressing earlier? That I got a wild hair at the last possible moment, cramming money into its lining even though it was uncomfortable as hell?

Does this mean things are looking up for me? Is

the universe, for once, blessing me with a freaking break, the kind I never get but which everyone else seems to?

I don't dare hope. I know better than that. I'm not a lucky girl.

My motto should be *what life giveth, it taketh away.* Right away. Without waiting or warning.

And yet here I am, sitting in a Target Starbucks, sipping a coffee exactly how I like it with non-fat milk and lots of sugar, wearing normal clothes that my ass is not hanging out of for a change.

Who knew these little things mattered so, so much?

For a moment, I am immersed in my old life. The one where I get up every day and open one of my bookkeeping texts first thing, absorbing as much as I can before heading to Pops's pawn shop to see what he needs help with that day. He's usually there before me, so on the way in, I pick up bagels and coffee after dropping my little sister at school.

I work a few hours and get back to the books. If I'm not meeting with my study buddy Luci, we at least have a Zoom call to go over our homework.

And then I have class in the evening. The highlight of my day. Or week. Or lifetime.

I've never been much of a student. Not because I

don't have the brains. I was just never all that interested.

That's behind me now.

For the first time in my life, thanks to my instructor and new BFF, I am getting A's. It feels so good. Like nothing I've ever experienced.

Never too late to redeem yourself, as my mother used to say.

I didn't understand what she meant by that, back when she was alive. Figured it was something she read in the Bible or one of her religion books. But I understand it now. I'm getting a second chance.

Or, I *was*.

Was Mother referring to my father when she said that? Did she feel he needed to step up to the plate in some areas? Was she acknowledging things I only became aware of as an adult?

And was he the cause of her death, as Niko and his brothers suspect?

The coffee hits my stomach hard, and the burn splashes to the back of my throat. I can't get sick here. Not in Target. Not when I have only minutes to figure out next steps.

One of the baristas, wiping down tables in anticipation of closing, peeks at me around the corner and smiles.

"Fifteen minutes, ma'am," she says politely.

"No problem," I say cheerfully.

On the surface, I'm just any other girl dressed casually, enjoying her coffee and staring at her phone. No one here knows what I've been through.

No one would believe it if I told them, anyway. I can scarcely believe it myself.

Kidnapped to pay my father's debts by some psycho organized crime trio of brothers who, by the way, are walking sex on a stick, who have enemies out the ass who are only too willing to show each other up by fighting over me.

Me.

I don't know which part of that scenario is most crazy, but I do find the most puzzling to be that anyone would look twice in my direction, never mind battle over who gets to 'own' me.

How about this, mother fuckers? *Nobody* gets to own me. And right now is when they start learning that.

If this shit show hadn't just become my life, I'd never believe it was possible.

A security guard making the rounds walks by me, having just gotten his own coffee. He cordially nods. Should I ask him for help?

Have him call the cops for me?

Sure. I could do that. If I want to see my father dead and my little sister soon to follow.

At that, I take a quick bite of scone to settle the nausea. It doesn't help and I wonder if I have time to purchase some Rolaids before the last cash register closes for the night.

That's when the harsh reality that I'm on my own lights me up—no cop can help me now, never mind a Target security guard.

Clarity.

A little, anyway. I have a next step.

Using my new phone, I dial one of the few numbers I have memorized.

"Victoria?"

There's a gasp on the other end of the line. "Oh my God. Is that you, Charleigh?"

My voice breaks when I hear hers. She's someone who cares about me. Someone who has been there for me, especially since my mother died.

"Y… yes, Vic. It's me. I need help."

CHAPTER TWO

Charleigh

Camping out at Victoria's was meant to be a short-term solution. I just didn't know how short-term.

She works for Pops, so anyone looking for me will certainly question her as soon as they finish with my father. But hers was the only place I could think to go that desperate night in Target. And a few days later, it's already time to move on.

So soon.

"What did they say? What did they want?" I ask.

She rushes to her apartment window and pulls the blinds closed, not that I'd gone anywhere near the windows in the three days I'd holed up there.

She paces, a hand on her forehead, inches from a

panic attack. I know this because my mother used to have them.

"They come by every day, asking the same questions. *Have you seen Charleigh? Where do you think she is?* I just follow your dad's lead and say I have no idea."

These men aren't stupid. They are messing with her. And doing a good job.

"Okay. Then why are you freaking *now?*"

"Because," she says, placing a hand on her abdomen like she's going to get sick, "I'm pretty sure they're following me. They don't believe me. We have to think of next steps, honey. I'm sorry."

A gut punch washes through me. I'm quite familiar with them these days. My new little friends.

I know what Victoria is saying—it's time for me to get the hell out of there.

Of course, the Alekseev brothers are looking for me. I am a *highly valuable asset,* as they so crudely put it. They're using me to pay off Pops's gambling debts. They're not about to let go easily. If ever.

No, those bastards will hunt me until my dying day if for no other reason that I made them look bad by escaping.

So, do I think for a moment they'll ever throw their hands up in the air like, *oh well, she's gone?* I am not that naïve.

Even if I were worth absolutely nothing in their estimation, they'd still be after me.

Because, pride.

It's not just about the money for them. To these toxically masculine alpha men, there is nothing more valued than their pride. I have no doubt my hitting the road struck them right where it hurts. They can't live with being bested. Tricked. Outmaneuvered.

Their egos are epic. Epic egos are fragile. Fragile egos are dangerous.

Too fucking bad.

They thought I was their property. They can think again.

As happy as I am to be out of their clutches, I have wondered these past few days exactly how things are going down at the club. Strange, I know. I wish Stacey still worked there, instead of disappearing like she did. She'd fill me in, I have no doubt, sharing anything she may have overhead about their plans to pursue me. And what they'll do when and if they find me.

Instead, I have only my imagination.

Which, unfortunately, has set my dreams on fire every single night since I left. I don't want to dream about the Alekseev brothers. I want to forget I ever knew them.

And yet.

At night, when it's dark and I feel safest, Niko, the nicest brother, pops up in my dreams. Tall and blond, looking nothing like the others, he is the literal embodiment of a betrayal, the weight of which he's carried all his life. Yet he's kind and gentle. Well, at least as kind and gentle as a Bratva member can be.

His brother Kir is a bit edgier, doing all he can to prolong the punishment he imposes on himself for losing his beloved. He beats himself up day and night for what happened to his Clara. He might hold forgiveness in his heart for other people, but he has none for himself. I honestly think the only time I've seen him laugh, really laugh, is when his brothers are busting his chops over the funny man bun he wears.

Last but not least is the severe Vadik. That's the best word I can think to describe him with. His face is in a permanent scowl, it seems, and he deftly plays the role of oldest brother, making decisions with breathtaking finality. That doesn't mean Kir and Niko don't question him. They do. But they are the only people who dare stand up to this man with the shaved head who would scare anybody in a dark alley.

In spite of myself, and how detestable I find them, these men inhabit my dreams. I'd give anything to be away from them, and yet they tease my thoughts without mercy, testing my resolve, my sanity, and my dignity.

What kind of bullshit is that?

Next morning, Victoria wakes me while it's still dark outside.

"Hey." My brain is foggy with drowsiness. "What's up? Did something happen?" As sleep slips away, alarm and anxiety take its place. My new normal. A permanent visitor that won't leave.

She takes a seat on the edge of my bed and smooths the hair off my face. Her touch takes me back to when I was a broken-hearted ten-year-old, unsure how I would live without my mother. It was so kind of Victoria to help my sisters and me back then, and here she is now, doing it again. There's no way I can ever thank her.

Except make her proud.

"No, nothing new," she whispers. "I have something for you, though," she says, handing me some folded tissue paper.

I don't even have to open it to know what it is.

It smells exactly like the powdery drugstore cologne my mother used to wear.

I loved that scent as a kid and a lump grows in my throat as I remember how, whenever I threw my arms around her, I'd bury my nose in her neck, breathing as deeply as possible.

I'll never forget that smell. It's a part of me just like my fingerprints are. I miss it to my core, just like I miss my mother. If she were still alive, I wouldn't be in the situation I am right now. I'd be breathing her cologne, live and in person.

My heart hurts as these thoughts rumble through my head. So, I push them away. Or, rather, try to.

Sometimes I succeed, sometimes I don't.

"It this what I think it is?" I ask in a hushed voice, swallowing down the lump in my throat.

I take the package she's handing me like it's a rare treasure. Which it is.

She nods. "Open it."

I unfold the yellowed tissue, and Mother's scent hits me so hard, tears fall anyway. "Oh my God, Vic."

I take a corner of delicate fabric, and let its folds unfurl between the two of us. When I do, I see there is more inside the paper, folded just as carefully.

"Mom's scarves," I whisper, fingering the fabric like priceless artifacts. "Wh… where did you get these?"

She unfolds a second one and lays it across the bed to admire. "Remember when your father had me clean out your mother's stuff way back when?"

I was young then, only ten years old, but I remember Victoria arguing with my father. He wanted all of Mother's things out of the house right after she died. Victoria had suggested keeping at least a few things, if for no other reason than for us girls, but Pops told her to mind her own business and finish the job.

"I put aside these things," Victoria says. "I knew you might like to have them someday. Your father has no idea. Just like he doesn't know about that necklace you have on."

Her eyes twinkle.

I touch the locket at my throat, something I had to swipe before Pops disposed of it, them pull another diaphanous scarf through my fingers. My mother didn't have many nice things, but her parents had given her silk scarves, something my father was never able to.

Perhaps that's why he wanted her belongings out of the house so quickly. They were a reminder of all he couldn't give her. And all he couldn't be for her.

And how he couldn't save her in the end.

"Thank you, Victoria," I whisper hoarsely, holding a fistful of the scarves up to my nose.

It's as if Mother is here in the room right now.

Victoria pats the bed, our reminiscing moment over. "Okay, Char. Here's what we're doing today. I'm taking Uber to work. You take my car, do what you have to, and head to the bus station. Leave the car there and get out of town, as fast and as far as possible. These men who are after you, they…"

Her voice trailed off as her eyes filled with tears.

I took her hand and squeezed it. "I know, Vic. I know how they are. As soon as school opens, I'll take the car to see Evie. Then I'll leave."

She nods. "Okay, honey. And know, I'm not kicking you out. We both knew you could hide here for only so long."

I throw my arms around her. "I know, Victoria. You saved me once, and you're saving me again. I don't know how I can thank you."

She looks at me. "You don't have to thank me. You never have to thank me. Your mother was my friend and I do these things for you girls in her honor."

CHAPTER THREE

CHARLEIGH

I have no idea how Evie's getting to school since I haven't been able to take her these past weeks, but I know she's resourceful enough to scare up rides if she needs them. And I'm right. I see her best friend's mom drop a carload of kids off at exactly seven fifteen a.m. I call to Evie just before she goes inside, after her friends already have.

The less attention I attract, the better.

She turns, and when she sees me, her face brightens. But only for a moment. Her relief is instantly replaced by her teenage scowl, and as she gets closer, I can see she's had her nose pierced.

Yup, she's about as unsupervised as I thought she'd be.

"Hey," she says coldly.

Really?

"Hey yourself."

She looks around the school parking lot like she's watching for someone. "Some guys came by, asking about you. They offered me money to contact them if I spoke to you." Her gaze is cold and indifferent.

Maybe she is as full of hate as she pretends to be.

"Are you going to take it?" I ask. "Are you going to tell them you saw me?"

She holds her chin up like she's a badass. "Maybe," she sniffs.

God, this child is hard to love sometimes. I'm ninety-nine percent sure she's bluffing. But that other one percent…

I push my fears away. She's my sister. She might be a monstrous ball of hormones, but she's still my sister.

I reach into my pocket and hand her a wad of twenties.

"What's this?" she asks, her face covered in bewilderment.

"Put it away," I say, gesturing with my chin. "Put it in your pocket. Don't show it to anyone and don't tell anyone about it. It's for emergencies only. Hide it and don't tell Pops."

Her bottom lip quivers as she takes in the seriousness of my tone. Thank God. I've reached her.

I press a small scrap of paper into her hand. "Hide this too. This is the number to my burner phone. Do not ever give it to anyone. Understand?"

Her big, overly made-up eyes are watering now, and a tear or two threatens to run down her pretty cheeks. Instead of the defiant teenager she was a few moments ago, she's once again my little sister, vulnerable and afraid. And hopelessly dependent on me.

It kills me. Just fucking kills me. That this kid has to suffer for all the bullshit the adults around her get themselves into. Life is so not fucking fair.

But I already know that.

I pull her into my arms, squeezing her until she protests. "I'll be in touch. Try to be good, honey."

"Wh… when will you be back?" she asks, trying to hide the break in her voice.

And now I'm trying to hide my own.

"I'm not sure. But I'll be in touch with you. No one else. Okay?"

She nods and I run back to the car while I have the courage to go.

CHAPTER FOUR

CHARLEIGH

I settle into the seat of one of the bus station's wooden benches, indentations worn into the wood from years of peoples' behinds sliding over them. The walls are of puke-y green cinder blocks. There is an ancient clock hanging on them, which, I realize when I check my burner phone, tells the wrong time.

My new hoodie is pulled tightly around my face, over the cap that partially shields my eyes. I am under no illusion there is anything remotely safe about where I am right now, despite my attempts at a disguise. In fact, I'm quite sure I'm not much more than a sitting duck. After all, if the guys are looking for me, isn't this one of the places I'm most likely to come?

But I won't be here long, if all goes according to plan.

The bus station is, I suppose, a pretty good cross-section of society. Of course, people with cars, or those who can afford air travel, have probably never seen the inside of one. But people like me, of less-than-middling means, populate bus stations everywhere. I look around, and while I don't know any of these people, I do know them. All of them.

So to speak.

In fact, I nod at one woman across the room who looks to be around my age, who's staring at me.

Shit. Why did I just do that?

I look at a board for the list of destinations the buses are heading to. North, south, east, and west—they're all available and within my budget.

And yet, I can't make a decision.

The woman across the room continues to stare at me, even while she lifts her phone to her ear for a call. Of course I can't hear what she's saying, but she puts her free hand over her mouth as if I might read her lips, nods, then puts her phone back in her pocket.

Never taking her eyes off me.

What the fuck?

I have an urge to cross the room and ask what

her problem is when I realize there's another clock behind me. That's what she's been watching.

Jesus, girl. Get a grip.

My mind wanders back to Evie's false bravado. She acts like she's so tough—hell, she probably even believes she is—but I know better. She's about as vulnerable as they come. She has a photo of Mother on her nightstand, and sometimes I can hear her talking to it. She even still keeps the teddy bear our mother got her on her bed, God forbid anyone ever touches it. You'd think it was made of gold.

Maybe to her, it is. I reach into the outer pocket of my backpack and finger Mother's scarves, and a whiff of her cologne wafts toward me.

I hate to admit it, but I no longer care what my running does to my father. He doesn't care what happens to me.

But Evie is a different story. Without the supervision she needs, she'll slip between the cracks of society like she never existed. Hell, I'm already holding on to her by the edges of my fingernails.

I look down at my burner phone as if someone might call me. But the only two people who have my number are Victoria and my sister. Vic won't call unless she absolutely has to, and Evie is in class right now.

I want so desperately to talk to someone.

Anyone. I've never felt so alone. I look up to see if the girl who was watching me might be open to a friendly conversation. But when I do, I find she's gone.

My heart slams into my chest, and every beat thumps with the same message.

She's with them. You'll never get away.

You are a fool. A little fool.

There is a bus leaving in two minutes. If I run, I can get on it. I'll sneak to the back and sink low in my seat. Hopefully no one will see me, and I'll be on my way.

But Evie's big, glossy eyes haunt me.

As do the touches of the Alekseev brothers.

Goddammit.

I dial Victoria. Hopefully, she's at the shop by herself and can speak freely.

But a man answers. A man I know. "Hello?" he barks.

It's Vadik. Vadik is answering the shop phone.

"Is that you, Charleigh? You'd better come clean, pretty girl. Because right now we have your dear friend with a gun to her head because she won't tell us where to find you. Here. Listen," he says.

Muffled screams come through the phone line and I know my journey is over. I have no options. I am going nowhere, escaping no one.

I'm stuck in the hellish world I thought I might be able to leave behind. There's no escape. There never was.

"You'd better decide quickly, honey. Time is running out for your friend." The malice in his words makes me tremble.

"Leave her alone," I growl.

Laughter explodes in my ear. He thinks this is funny. He thinks I'm funny.

I don't.

I grind my teeth in anger, anger I need to hold on to. "You bastard. If you hurt her, I'll kill you. I will find a way, and I will kill you."

I shock myself with the vehemence of my words. But I mean them like I've never meant anything in my life.

"Well then, pretty girl," he croons, "you'd best return *home*. To your *new home* that is. And then your loved ones will be safe. Including… your little sister. What's her name again? Evie, I think. So cute with her new nose piercing…"

I hang up the call and race out of the station, past Victoria's car, to the first cab I see.

She can pick up her car tomorrow.

If she's still alive.

CHAPTER FIVE

VADIK

We seldom kill men from opposing Bratva factions. It just doesn't accomplish much, serving only to piss off the *Pakhan*, and to prolong a vicious, endless conflict with no solution.

It's common sense, really. We kill one of theirs, they kill one of ours. And so on, and so forth, until things are a real fucking mess and there are dead bodies everywhere, drawing attention to ourselves and weakening the organization. While this is one of the first things Papa taught me when I was coming up and he was teaching me the ropes, my brothers and I have seen firsthand what happens when things get out of control.

And when the *Pakhan* is pulled in, you know shit is getting real.

But sometimes an exception is made. Today may be one of those days.

Our interrogation is not going smoothly, which is making me unhappy. Very unhappy. I already have enough on my mind with Charleigh's disappearance. But that will be resolved in time, just like this little issue will.

Kir and Niko are hanging back, standing guard, among other things, while I chat with the gentleman from our rival faction, the one we believe is the mastermind behind our missing shipment of firearms.

Mastermind may be giving him too much credit. It's not hard to bribe the assholes running our country's ports in order to see that a shipment or two are *misdirected* or even *lost,* terms shippers love to use. But what they really mean is that some motherfucker helped himself to our cargo. Of course, this doesn't happen without help. A lot of help.

The details of which we are trying to untangle today.

One of the guys on our payroll, put in place to watch over our assets, heard from someone who heard from someone that a shipment of guns was coming in. Our guy played along with the thieves to collect as much information as he could until they got suspicious of him. He then disappeared. I hope he's alive but the chances of that are not good. Informants take off all the time when there's too much heat on them but more often than not they wind up dead. Sometimes they are found, sometimes not.

With our intel having reached a literal dead end, we planted a new guy. And he led us to our friend here, whom we're having a chat with today. Our new plant deserves a bonus. A big one.

The man is tied to a chair in the middle of the room. I hate this sort of bullshit drama. It looks like something out of a cheesy mafia movie. But hell, sometimes we really do business this way. Tying guys to chairs and 'encouraging' them to talk is actually quite effective.

Usually. But it's not working too well today.

It's the same old story. He claims to know nothing. But that is a lie. How do I know? Because I can read people, and this asshole's an open book. If the sweat dripping down his temples and his trembling lips don't say enough, his darting eyes and shaking have all but given him away.

He's our guy. He knows we know. And he knows he's as good as dead. Yet he won't tell us where our shit is. Someone's holding something over him. Something big. So big, he'd rather die at our hands than divulge his secret. They probably threatened to kill his family or some such.

Happens all the time.

Niko is in charge of our shipping business. And, as new as he is to it, as the youngest brother and newest one to the business, he does a damn good job. But this one incident was something I wanted to handle myself. To send a message. That the Alekseevs won't be fucked with.

I have a feeling everyone in our world is about to get that message, loud and clear.

Kir, on the other hand, runs our card games and cleans the cash through our liquor stores. He's the best at what he does, and while I hate to drag him away from his work for even an hour, I needed both brothers today to present a united front as we drive home our message.

We're all good in our roles. We learned from the best—Papa—which is why we have the most successful businesses in our region.

And why they are also the most coveted. I can't blame the others. I mean, who wouldn't want to grab a piece of what the Alekseevs have?

Unfortunately for them, such ambitions don't usually play out well.

Envy will do that.

When we arrived at our warehouse to interrogate this guy, we were greeted by a couple new hires working security, who looked too young to even have hair on their balls. Fucking pisses me off. I give one of our right-hand men the authority to build his team, and he brings in rookies like this?

Is it that hard to find a few grownups?

But I'll take care of that later. I kick the kids out, telling them to stand watch outside the building. Problem is, if anything goes wrong, they'll be the first ones taken out. Which would be a pity.

Thank God I brought my brothers. The youngsters look like they can barely hold their guns, much let shoot with any level of accuracy.

I make a mental note to talk to our manager later.

Folks in our business are subject to a fast and furious culling. One of three things happens to the majority of them. They either succeed, end up with a bullet between their eyes, or they can't hang and split. Those who make it through the early days are usually with us for life, guaranteed to make a lot of money and live well. That is, unless they're offed before their time.

Something we are all well aware of.

After a customary sweep of the building—it might be our property but vigilance always pays off—we get down to work.

I grab a seat so I'm eye-to-eye with the man tied to the chair in front of me. There is already a puddle of urine under his chair, which annoys me because it stinks. If there's anything I hate, it's the pungent smell of piss. Hopefully, I won't be here long. I doubt he'll be generous with the information he's withholding, but I'll give him a chance first.

"One more time. Who's behind stealing our shipment?" I ask patiently. Even politely. The man knows I'm serious. There's no need to growl or shout.

His mouth distorts and when he opens it to speak, a string of spittle stretches between his lips. There is dried blood on his temple where the team who brought him in knocked him around and as he tries to speak, a tooth tumbles out of his mouth.

This guy is fucked. He knows he's fucked.

In spite of his silence, my brothers and I are pretty positive he was hired by someone who was hired by someone who was hired by our nemesis Dimitri Yegorov. Reason being, that while Dimitri no doubt wants to fuck with us, there is no way he has the brains to pull off a sophisticated heist. He does know, however, to create a long enough chain of transactions so that the bastard on the end doesn't know where it all started. That's how he keeps his own ass safe.

At least that's what he thinks.

The man I'm looking at is giving up nothing, and this day has turned into a colossal waste of my time. Plus, my goddamn migraines are back, probably not helped by all the drinking I've been doing, and I don't have my pills with me.

This, and the absence of Charleigh has put me off my game. There was a time when I could look at a man and he'd spill his guts to me. Tell me more than I ever wanted to know. But now? This pathetic man is looking me right in the eye, ready to die with his secrets.

He has balls, I'll give him that.

The tension back at the club has been unbearable. Not surprisingly, Dominika was the first to wash her hands of any responsibility with regard to Charleigh's *escape* as everyone's been calling it, even though Dominika is the goddamn club manager. And for a while, we suspected Dimitri's making a scene, distracting everyone at the start of the auction, was a set-up so Charleigh could get out. But after surveilling him and finding no sign of her in his possession, his name was crossed off the list as much as he would have loved to be the one who snagged her.

It seems Charleigh saw an opportunity and grabbed it. The bouncer left his post to tend to Dimitri, and the girl was home free.

I have to admit, it stings a little. Actually, a lot. My brothers and I had plans for her, and they did not include her going home with anyone other than the three of us. Not Dimitri, not Alexei, not some Saudi prince—no one. She was safe from all those bastards. None of them would win her at auction. We had everything fixed, and we were to be the winners. We were protecting her. We wanted her.

Some might say we *needed* her.

We just didn't get the chance to tell her, and she ran before we could.

After the auction was cancelled and we sent everyone home—a bunch of very unhappy club members, but what can you do?—Kir exploded on me, backed up by Niko. First time my brothers have ever come down on me.

I should have told her the plan, they said. She never would have taken off.

To that, I say, fuck off. Of course, she would have left, regardless. She doesn't want to be with us guys. We stand for everything she doesn't. She could never adapt to our lifestyle.

And now that means we have to take her misdeeds out on her father's hide. We can't just let it go. What would that look like?

With one last look at the man I'm questioning, I get up from my chair and head to the door. "Call the guys in from outside. Let them take care of this joker."

Niko and Kir usher the kids back inside and put

them to work. I wait in the back of the limo. I'm tired. So tired.

Five minutes later, my brothers join me in the car and we head out.

"Can they handle it? The kids?" I ask.

Kir nods. "They know what to do."

We'll make an example of that guy back there, and how he was loyal to the wrong people. Send a message loud and clear there's no going up against the Alekseevs.

CHAPTER SIX

VADIK

Niko props his feet up on the limo seat next to me, his dress shoes the epitome of perfection, like all his clothes. He's the only man I've ever known to never get a scuff on his shoes.

Fucking weird, if you ask me.

"Put your feet down, you slob," I say. I don't care how nice his shoes are. That's disgusting.

He ignores me. "Somebody's in a shit mood."

I pull my phone out and start scrolling. My head is pounding and I don't want to talk.

"Seriously, man," Kir adds. "Who knew Vadik could fall so hard?" he says, goading me.

I glare at my brothers, who are trying to push my buttons. They are succeeding.

"When we get her back…" I murmur. I don't

finish because I'm not sure what I'll do when we get her back.

Kir leans forward. "Man. You can't even say her name."

This enrages me. I close my eyes because my head is seconds from exploding. My blood pressure spikes and I grit my teeth so hard it hurts. I want to punch my brother. No, I actually want to strangle him. I don't, of course. But the temptation is real.

These guys are the only people on earth I tolerate disrespect from. Anyone else, and the punishment is swift and painful.

Charleigh's punishment will be swift and painful. It will hurt her, but will hurt me more. And yet I will carry it out without hesitation. That is, when we get her back. And we will.

"Don't ride me, Kir. I'm not in the mood," I growl.

"You're not going to hurt her. I'm telling you that now," Niko says.

I'm going to kill both my brothers if they don't shut up.

"I'll kill her," I warn. "That's what she deserves for what she's done."

Kir and Niko look at each other, saying nothing. They know better than to try and reason with me when I'm in one of my moods. They also know I'm blowing hot air. I won't kill her. I would never kill her.

Niko shrugs. "C'mon, Vadik. Are you really surprised she bolted? She's not an idiot. Of course she was going to try."

Kir nods. "She's *one* chick. One of many. When it comes down to it, who really cares? Yeah, she got one over on us. Big fucking deal. Look at all the others who didn't."

It only takes one, I want to say. It only takes one to fuck everything up.

We're the talk of the region now. Our very own auction asset, a beautiful young woman coveted by men around the world, up and walked right out our door, right under our noses. We could have made millions off her and her precious virginity, which I'd actually already snagged for myself, not that the fuckers who wanted her would ever know.

How do these two fools, my brothers Kir and Niko, think this makes us appear to the other factions? The rumors are going crazy according to my sources, and we look like fucking idiots.

Yeah, we've made steps to ensure this doesn't happen again. We got a new bouncer for one, and from now on, our 'high-value' girls will have their own personal security.

But the thing that makes me the most angry is

that I miss her. It makes me angry with her, and angrier with myself. Goddammit, I hate that I miss this woman who ran off with my heart in her pocket. She didn't give us a chance. She didn't give me a chance. And I'm so pissed I let her do that to me, let her get under my skin.

We were going to do right by her. She left before we could tell her that.

We'll get her back and when we do, she'll tell us who helped her escape. Because I know she couldn't have gotten away and hidden on her own. It's impossible. We have tentacles throughout the region. We know everything that happens. And when we're looking for someone and sound the 'alarm,' so to speak, our contacts come through for us. Every time. Without fail.

She will be back in our clutches in due time. I know she will.

My level of fury scares me.

But I will not indulge my rage right now, much as I want to. I could kill one hundred men with my bare hands, and still want to kill a hundred more. I will bottle this thunderous energy for later use, for a more appropriate time, after Charleigh is found. And if she dares to leave us again, I will destroy everyone and everything she's ever cared about.

Then I will destroy her. Because if I don't, she'll destroy me.

CHAPTER SEVEN

Vadik

Dominika meets my brothers and me as we return to the club, and rides the elevator with us.

"Anything new?" Kir asks.

She smiles coyly. I hate it when she does that.

First, *coy* does not work on Dominika. She's anything but. She's more of a mankiller, and pretending to be otherwise does not suit her. She looks ridiculous.

Because I'm in such a shit mood, I pretend she's not standing three feet away from me, and let my brothers do the talking.

"Well, there are a couple things," she teases, running her nails down Kir's jacket sleeve.

He diplomatically removes himself from her

touch with so much skill, she doesn't even notice his revulsion.

"Are you going to fill us in? Or should we guess? Maybe play a game of charades?" he snaps.

Her chin twitches the tiniest amount as she realizes she's pushing her luck.

She puts her hands on her hips, back to her usual ball-busting self. "First of all, there are a bunch of members still bitching and moaning about the auction."

Tell me something I don't know.

"And second, the security guys at your compound just called. An unexpected visitor has shown up at your home." Her dark eyes glitter with excitement. Seriously, she looks so happy to be sharing something she heard before us, I think she's about to come in her panties.

We walk down the hall, unwilling to beg her to share her precious information. When she realizes this, she trots to keep up, defeated we didn't let her wield any power over us.

"Don't you want to know who showed up at the compound, boys?" she taunts.

She really is not getting the message.

"If you're going to ask us to beg for it, no. I will just call security myself to see what's going on," I say, dialing.

"Suit yourself, guys. But I can tell you the same thing they will."

"And what's that, Dominika?" Kir asks in a tired voice.

"Charleigh has returned. Your little Charleigh. She's back."

CHAPTER EIGHT

"Nice of you to stop by," Kir growls

He glares at me with venomous eyes. Vadik stands clear across my bedroom room, gazing out the window as if I'm not worth looking at. Niko scrolls through his phone like he has more important things to do.

And the punishment commences.

I sit on the edge of my bed, where I've been waiting for the guys since the security guards brought me to my room and locked me in. I knew it would be only a matter of minutes until the brothers got here. I brushed my teeth and fixed my hair. Swiped on a little lip gloss and ran my mother's scarves through my fingers for strength. I wanted to be ready.

While I'm enduring their silent treatment, I think through everything that led me back here, everything that happened in the last hour of my life.

As the taxi I grabbed at the train station approaches the Alekseev compound, I have the driver drop me a couple blocks away in case I change my mind about returning. Wearing my backpack, I slowly walk through the tony neighborhood with its massive homes and manicured lawns, the huge old oaks overhead making it all so wholesome.

Isn't this how everyone wants to live? In a pretty house in a nice neighborhood?

And yet, what lay ahead has me terrified. More than terrified. I have no idea what the guys will do when I surrender myself to them.

But I know what they'll do if I *don't*. And I can't let that happen to my sister. There's Pops, of course, but the more I think about it, the more I'm okay with leaving him on his own.

Life right now is not offering me many options. I need to set priorities. And Evie is it.

As I head toward the Alekseev's, a shiny black SUV speeding down the street and around a corner startles me. I can't see whether it's going to their compound, and whoever's in it probably won't recognize me, anyway, not with my cap pulled low and a hoodie drawn around it. I force myself to relax, at least as much as I can. I'm walking with a slow shuffle, and figure I probably look like some kid just coming home from school.

Still, the passing car jolts me, whether it's going to the Alekseev's or not. If I don't return to them, every shiny black SUV I see for the rest of my life will cause the same pit in my stomach I feel right now. Can I live like that?

Sure, I could escape, but what kind of escape would it be, where my every waking moment is haunted with fear? That sounds like the worst prison of all.

As I meander, still torn about returning or continuing to run, I see a path in the thick woods between two houses. It twists out of sight and for a moment, I consider running down it and getting lost. But then a vision of my little sister, back when Victoria picked us up from school the day our mother was murdered, appears in my mind and I'm reminded why I'm doing what I can.

When Victoria collected us that day, we didn't know anything yet. But even in the car, Evie looked comatose. As if she knew something had happened, and that our lives were about to change in ways both minute and unimaginable.

As soon as we got home, I spread out my home-work on the kitchen table, eager to finish it before

Mother got home to check it. Evie, who usually played with her dolls while I kept an eye on her, curled up on the sofa and started sucking her thumb, something she hadn't done in years.

I didn't think anything of it at the time, but she's always been sensitive. I wonder if on some level she knew what was going on?

I'm at the end of my journey, short-lived though it was. I round a corner and consider the Alekseev's property before me, surrounded with tall, forbidding wrought iron that I know is electrified. All the property's structures are obscured by huge old oaks. From the street you can't see a thing.

Except for a little guard shack that looks like no more than a shed where you might keep your garbage cans.

I know differently.

I walk up to the shack, hoping I don't surprise anyone and end up with my head shot off. I knock and hear some rustling and clicking inside, and then a speaker comes alive.

"Yes?"

As if their cameras can't see me.

"Hi. It's Charleigh Gates. I've come to… see the guys."

Inside of about ten seconds flat, I am whisked onto the property, led across the yard with a tight grip on the back of my hoodie, brought upstairs, and locked in my old room, where not a thing has been moved since I was last there.

Well. That was easy.

And now here I am, facing the guys after four days of being on the lam. If they are happy to see me, it sure doesn't seem like it. Guess the feeling's mutual, though. I'm not that thrilled to see them, either.

"I… I…" I fumble. I want to say something but am not sure what.

Should tell them it's nice to see them?

Should I tell them I'm sorry?

Should I tell them I appreciate being back on the compound?

I don't bother, because none of these things are true. I'm here for my sister.

"Not a word from you," Kir growls before I can say anything else.

Really? Is what I did so bad? I didn't hurt anyone. I didn't steal anything. The only victims of my 'crime' are my family.

Oh, and I guess the old Alekseev pride.

Yeah, they're pissed I bailed on them. Well, they can fucking get over it.

"Take your clothes off and get in the shower. Scrub yourself clean," he barks.

I stand up from the bed, happy to comply. "Um, well, could I have a little privacy, please?" I snip, gesturing toward my door in the most polite way I can think to ask them to leave.

"No," Vadik snaps, slowly turning to face me.

The expression on his face can be described with no other word than *disgust.*

"Okay," I shrug, probably pissing them off further with my indifferent manner.

I pull off my hoodie, jeans, and everything else I'm wearing under the watchful gaze of all three guys, and saunter toward my bathroom. I leave the door wide open and take a long, leisurely, steaming hot shower.

When I am done, I wrap my hair in a fluffy white towel, and return to the room, dripping wet and soaking the carpet under our feet.

Naked.

I put my hands on my hips. "Happy now?"

Their expressions make clear I'm not in just any old trouble with them. What I did was massively public and no doubt embarrassed the shit out of them.

I can hear it now. *If we can't control a woman, how can we control our business?*

Their authority has been disrespected. This

weakens their power, at least in the eyes of their club members and everyone they do business with.

And yet, if I had the chance to do it again, to take off, I would. I had to try. I would be a fool not to.

"We knew where you were the whole time," Niko says, his tone not mean or angry, but just flat. Depressed. As if I hurt his feelings.

"Then why did you ask who helped me?"

His eyes rove my naked body and while I'm parading around unclothed out of defiance, I have to admit, I like his gaze on me. It feels good. Strong.

These guys think I have no power in this situation?

Think again, my friends.

"The cab driver works for us," Niko says. "He called when he dropped you at Target, and followed you to Victoria's."

Wow. The bastard. He seemed so nice. Why did he even pretend to help me? Was it fun for him, in some sad, sick way? Get one over on the pathetic girl running for her life? Lead her on, give her some hope there's a better life for her out there if only she can get away without a trace?

He probably got a good laugh at my expense, and a nice bonus from the Alekseevs. Jesus, is there anyone in this town these guys don't own?

Is everyone for freaking sale? And if so, why am I

only just now learning this is the way the world works? It's like I missed the memo or something.

That life sucks and by the way, so do all the people in it.

Bastards. The whole thing, the entire time I was gone, was just a contest of wills. They let me sweat for days, wondering if they'd find me when they knew where I was all along. They just let me stew in my worry while they lie in wait, like hungry spiders.

I yank the towel off my hair, running my fingers through my tangled strands. I'd like to pull on my thick, fluffy robe, but I continue to stand there, naked and rebellious. "Victoria is very important to my family. If you do anything to her—"

Kir laughs. "You'll what, Charleigh?"

He walks toward me with a menacing swagger. But I don't back down. I hold my chin up and pull my shoulders back. I don't care if I'm not dressed. I won't be intimidated.

I hold out my hands. "I'll cut my wrists open and bleed out all over the place. A lot of good I'll do you dead, huh?"

Kir's jaw twitches and I see I've hit a nerve. "Ballsy, pretty girl. That's a ballsy threat."

"Don't make me do it. Because I will," I whisper as he gets nearer.

"You shouldn't think thoughts like that, pretty

girl. They're too grim for you. You don't live in the same darkness my brothers and I do. Don't threaten such things."

I shrug. "You don't think I'll do what I say? Why wouldn't I? What else do I have to live for? Nothing around here," I scoff, gesturing around my fancy room.

So what if they've hooked me up with luxurious surroundings? That counts for nothing when you're imprisoned. Hell, the room could be dripping in gold and I still wouldn't want to be here against my will.

Do they really think I'll do backflips over the material comforts they've provided? Like that will make up for all they've taken from me?

I thought these men were smart.

I glance over at Vadik, whose eyes are wide. Did I get him with my threat? Have I finally gotten under someone's skin?

You'll pay for that, his expression says.

I keep my chin up to hide the sadness that begins to trickle over me. Defiance, bravery, boldness— they're getting me nowhere. The futility of my situation, a situation so beyond my control, crushes me like a thousand-pound weight. My eyes water but I won't cry. Not in front of them. I won't give them the satisfaction.

60

CHAPTER NINE

CHARLEIGH

Niko takes a seat at the end of the bed. "Come here."

Sighing, I walk over to him because what else am I going to do. He grabs my arms. Before I realize what's happening, I'm sprawled across his lap with my ass in the air. Vadik and Kir move behind me to enjoy the view.

It's not like they haven't seen my behind before, so I'm not sweating that. What I am sweating, is the beating I'm pretty sure I'm about to get.

What is it with these guys and their spankings?

As if Niko can read my mind, he explains. "This is not the most painful thing we can do to you. Not by a long shot. But it's humiliating, to be spanked like a little child. It's demeaning, and you will not enjoy it."

I hear a belt unbuckling and the scrape of leather against fabric as it's yanked out of belt loops. I can't see behind me, of course, but my ears are telling me all I need to know.

Niko inches my legs apart a bit and I know my most private parts are exposed.

Fuckers. They think they can own me?

My sad resignation blossoms into anger, anger that I desperately need and that empowers me. From my prone position on Niko's lap, I flail my arms, hitting him wherever I can with my closed fists.

Holding me in place, he restrains my hands behind my back. So much for my protest. I hear a *whoosh* as he winds up his now-free arm and brings his palm down on the flesh of my ass.

I shriek loud enough to be heard down the street. But it doesn't matter who hears me. No one will help anyway.

"Stop it. Do you hear me? Stop this bullshit, or things will get much worse," he hisses.

Behind me, I can hear the other two tittering.

Fuckers.

"Do you hear me?" he growls, using a fistful of my hair to yank my head back, arching me into a very uncomfortable position.

"Y… yes," I manage to sputter.

He releases my hair and my head drops back down. The only thing I can move are my legs, so I start kicking my feet.

Another *whoosh* and I brace myself. The smack I get this time is on the same butt cheek, I guess for maximum pain infliction and by God, it works like a charm. The smack is quick and loud but the follow-on burn remains, fingers of pain reaching through my battered bottom and to the rest of my body like every inch of me is being whipped. I gasp for air but can't seem to catch up and end up panting like a dog.

It seems as good a time as any to bargain, but the pain has taken away my ability to speak and all I can do is sputter. The guys chatter behind me, but I can't make out their words, the blood pulsing in my ears is so loud.

But I do make out one thing.

"Go ahead, Kir," Niko says.

That's when a slicing agony flays my other ass cheek, so deep and excruciating I scream the scream of someone in the depths of hell with flames licking off chunks of their flesh.

In a split moment of lucidity, I wonder if the household staff can hear and if they might come to my aid. Or at least call the police. But the reality is, the police are probably on the Alekseev payroll like everyone else I come across. And the household staff? Their loyalty is certainly not devoted to the likes of me. They not only want to keep their jobs but also want to stay alive. Helping me will not accomplish either.

Another vicious stroke tortures me. My screams echo pitifully, and no one cares, I know. Not a single person anywhere. Tears of anger drip from my eyes to the floor beneath me. Why me? I ask for the hundredth time. I want the universe to tell me what I did that was so bad that this is what my life has turned into.

I know life is not fair. I've seen it. I've lived it. But does it have to be *this* shitty?

Are there no fucking limits?

I need to remember this anger so I can conjure it later and put it to good use. But for now, I'm just a pathetic ball of tears and snot bent over a handsome, suited man's lap with my privates exposed for the world to see, getting my ass whipped, and I can't do a damn thing about it.

What these guys are turning me into breaks my heart. I'm becoming *like* them, living for revenge and all the ways I might carry it out. They're wrenching the last crumb of humanity from me and I'm afraid I'm becoming as hateful and dangerous as they are.

Like they've taken my *soul* from me because it was the last thing left they hadn't destroyed.

Kir whips my ass a couple more times and by some grace of God, I'm getting numb. My throat hurts from screaming, so I'm left with delirious little moans, my head bobbing reflexively with every strike.

"That'll teach her," one of them says with quiet satisfaction.

But they are not done yet.

Of course not.

Someone grabs the raw flesh of my ass and squeezes it in his fists, like the day is not complete without one, final parting shot. I raise my limp head and scream through it, and when the greedy hands release me, the pain somehow gets even worse, like they've dribbled caustic acid in my wounds.

"St… stop. Please stop," I mumble.

My words are ignored as two fingers slide between my legs while someone's lips brush my tortured ass. I'm wet, soaked in fact, and I'm more angry than ever that my body has betrayed me this way.

What the fuck? I am in excruciating pain from a spanking, and my vagina is thinking it's fun time?

Goddammit.

The same hand exploring me swirls around my

clit and the sensation is almost too much, mixed with the pain of my tender ass cheeks. I'm breathing hard again, dizzy from not only my head hanging low but also the collision of too many sensations at once.

I don't think I'll survive this. Which would honestly be for the best.

A hand soothes my lower back, careful to avoid my raw behind, and two fingers explore my opening. In spite of myself, and that I would rather be dead at that moment, I involuntarily push back. I want more. More pleasure, so I can forget the pain.

"Baby likes it," a deep voice whispers.

I suppose I could distinguish among the guys' voices, but that requires energy I do not have. All my focus now is on my core, the center of my being, and the pleasure that could possibly erase at least part of the agony I'm in.

I moan softly, humping the hand that's finger-fucking me. I have no shame at this moment, begging like a dog in heat, and yet the fingers inside me stop where they are, teasing me, prolonging the torture—this time, a different kind of torture—as if I'm to beg harder before I'm given what I really need.

"Isn't that nice, pretty girl?" Niko asks.

At least I think it's Niko.

"Y… yes. Please. I want… more."

"One sec. I'm picking you up, baby," a voice murmurs in my ear.

Moving from a bent position to a straight one reactivates the burn of my painful flesh, and I squirm violently, searching for a better position that alleviates my pain.

There is none.

I try to get my feet under me but my legs are useless, so I fall into the arms that pick me up like I weigh nothing. I am laid back on my bed, someone gently pushing a pillow under my lower back, raising my hips as if…

As if what?

A mouth descends on my privates before I can get my breath or even look around, and my eyes are closed again, my hips grinding against the source of pleasure, desperately demanding anything these men are willing to give me.

The tongue in my pussy laps me from clit to ass, where it lingers, poking at my rosebud, then back to my clit. Someone takes my legs—or is it *two someones?*—and pulls them back nearly until my knees are next to my ears.

I'm open, as open as I've ever been and I want it, I want to be fucked. I want to be fucked until it hurts so I feel alive and can forget my pain and anger, and how the life that's stretched out before me is not much more than a big, black ugly hole.

CHAPTER TEN

*K*IR

I run my tongue between Charleigh's cunt lips, lapping at her slick excitement, and bury my tongue as deeply inside her as I can. I want to taste every part of her. I've been waiting for this.

I know Vadik had her first. He admitted as much. And that's fine. It's not like it's a goddamn contest among my brothers and me. I just hope he was nice to her, and not his usual asshole self.

But today's a new day and as incredible as Charleigh feels, tastes, and smells, I can't help but hate myself a bit for the whipping I gave her. I was acting on behalf of the three of us brothers, it's true, but I let my anger get away from me and probably went too long and too hard. Vadik had to stop me before I flayed the actual flesh off her ass.

Something I've done before. And don't want to do again.

I was angry when she left during the auction, when she ran the moment we weren't looking, leaving us behind like goddamn chumps. Hell, I still *am* angry. Maybe more so than even my brothers. She has no idea what danger she put herself in by running. She has no idea how many of our rivals would have loved to pick her up and dangle her before us Alekseevs, like a piece of meat before a starving lion.

They know she is valuable to us. They don't know just how valuable.

Each smack against her ass moments ago was a relief, bleeding off my anger in a strange, sick satisfaction, like some sort of drug or maybe the first swig of a really good whiskey after a bad fucking day. It goes down like a burning river that quickly cools, spreading a sense of well-being, relaxing the mind and body. Problems scatter. Anger dissipates. To get through the day, I relied on this for a whole year after Clara died. The drinking, no the beatings. Still do, more often than I should.

I'm not proud of depending on such outlets for my emotions. It is what it is.

When I'd all but taken my thirst for revenge against Charleigh out on her ass, I scooped her from

Niko's lap and I found she was good and wet and ready for some healing. Her ass will hurt tomorrow and probably the next day too, possibly too much to even soak in the bathtub for relief.

But I bet she never fucking leaves again.

And now I'm preparing her tight pussy for my big, fat cock.

She moans softly as my tongue moves from her asshole to her pretty cunt, to her hard clit, and back again. Her sounds drill my brain and soon she's all I can hear, see, taste, and smell.

I run my hand under her ass and she gasps, snapping me out of my trance. "It's okay," I soothe. "The punishment is over."

I press my thumb into her clit like it's a fucking elevator button and she convulses lightly, dropping her head back. But I don't let her come. Not yet.

My brothers hold Charleigh's legs open and I reach up to pull her nipples.

"What do you want, pretty girl?" I ask.

"I… I want to come. I need to come…" she murmurs.

My cock is so hard it's about to burst out of my trousers. If I don't come in my pants first, like a goddamn teenage boy.

She shifts her hips to rub against the leg of my

trousers. I don't think she even realizes she's doing it, she's in such a trance.

"How do you want it, baby?"

"Your cock…" she stammers, like she's not used to saying the word. "I want you to… give me your cock."

Music to my ears.

I open my trousers just enough to free myself. I'm so insane with lust for this woman I won't take the time to kick off my shoes or even remove my clothing. I just pull out what I need to satisfy myself and this woman at this moment because that's all I care about.

The rest of the world could implode because all I want is to bury myself in her pretty pussy.

I notch myself at her opening and press until just my head pops in. She gasps from the stretch, clearly unaccustomed to anything in her sweet pussy, and I lean over her, stroking stray hairs off her forehead and brushing my lips over hers.

I know I need to be patient. Give her time. My desperate need to unwind all the anger and tension I carry should not be taken out on her.

She squirms to take more of me.

"Baby wants my cock? You want some cock?" I breathe in her ear.

"Please, Kir, please," she begs while I slide into her until my balls slap her ass.

She screams and then groans and as I hold myself inside her, and she tries to buck her hips under my weight.

"Fuck me, Kir, fuck me," she whispers.

I slide in and out, into a pussy that's gripping me so hard it almost hurts.

Or is it my backed-up balls?

She calls my name over and over while I stroke her insides, holding myself above her with one hand and circling her hard clit with the other. Her nails dig into my back as an orgasm rips her apart, leaving her screaming, flailing, and convulsing.

I drive into her one last time and my own explosion moves from my balls through my cock, and I fill her with my cum.

When I breathe again, my brothers let her legs go and I pull out, watching a few drops of my cum seep out of her well-fucked pussy and onto the bed below.

CHAPTER ELEVEN

Her eyes are closed tightly, and even when I kiss them, I can't get her to look at me. "You okay, baby?" I ask.

She turns to her side and rolls into a ball.

Really?

After all that, she doesn't feel the depth of our connection? What in the fucking hell?

"Your brothers left?" she asks.

I look around, only vaguely aware of my surroundings. "Yeah. I guess."

"Figures," she says quietly.

"What's that supposed to mean?" I ask, buckling my trousers.

She shakes her head, still not looking at me. "I know you guys. I know how you are."

Her words hit me like a spear. Without even completing her thought, I know what she's getting at.

"You don't know everything, Charleigh," I say, pulling a comforter up to her shoulders.

The bedroom door opens and my brothers return, Niko with tea and Vadik with an armful of towels.

Perfect timing.

She cranes her neck with surprise and leans up, unable to fully sit, and accepts tea from Niko. She puts her nose into the hot steam and closes her eyes, inhaling deeply.

"I brought you a couple warm towels," Vadik says with his usual gruffness.

Shit, I wish he could turn it off, at least once.

Charleigh looks up at him, I could swear with hurt in her eyes, and accepts them, laying them on the bed next to her.

"Thank you. I was just telling Kir I know what you guys are about. You play with my emotions, and then are willing to sell me like a common whore. That's why I left, you know. That, and the need to look after my sister. Not that you would care," she adds, looking straight into her tea.

Niko sighs, carefully choosing his words like he

always does, but Vadik huffs and storms out of the room.

After all this, she has no idea how we feel. Well, fuck all.

She turns to Niko and me. "Promise me, promise that no matter what happens to me, you will always look after my sister Evie. If I'm gone, she'll have no one. Not a soul on this earth to look after her." Her voice cracks at her last words, and the pain of loving someone so much you'd die for them is evident on her face.

And washes over me.

I know what it's like. I do. If only the car accident had taken my life instead of Clara's. I'd give anything for that. For a do-over of that night.

And yet here I am, subjected to a life on earth without her, ready to suffer until the end of my days.

But I can do some good. I can help Charleigh. In fact, I already have, more than she knows.

Vadik might still be pissed, and Niko is silently dealing with his feelings in his own way, but I'm being honest with Charleigh. She deserves that much.

We never had the chance to tell her she wasn't going to be sold at auction. That we were protecting her, keeping her from anyone else, whether Alexei, Dimitri, or the Saudis, from winning her.

We had no intention of letting any of them take her away. Because we want her for ourselves.

She was supposed to know this. She *should have* known this. I insisted to Vadik that we tell her. But he wanted to hold back to keep her on edge until the very last minute. It was the only way we'd be able to pull it off.

And then she left.

I'd be lying if I didn't say I was hurt when she split. Angry, too, that she was putting herself in danger, as well as casting a pall on the Alekseev businesses.

Who is this woman, I asked myself? She has no hold over me. She's nothing more than an asset being used to right her old man's wrongs. But that changed, and quickly.

My brothers and I discussed how we couldn't let her go and then put a plan in motion. A plan that went sideways when Charleigh decided to bolt.

After everyone had either arrived at the auction, or dialed in via the internet, we were going to let the bidding start. Yeah, we could have cancelled it altogether but after the buzz we'd created, we risked pissing off our members.

And looking pussy whipped.

Not a good look in our business.

So, we guys were joining the bidding, something

we seldom did. And because it was our auction, we were going to win.

It's that simple.

Only problem is, we didn't tell Charleigh in time.

Which was a big, fat, fucking mistake.

"I'm sorry, Charleigh," Niko says.

"For what?" she snaps, turning her back to us.

"We should have told you. We never were going to sell you. You were always going to be protected," I say. "You ran before we could fill you in on the plan."

She snorts and shakes her head. "Yeah, right. You guys are so full of shit."

Neither of us says anything until she turns over in bed to face us.

"What the hell are you talking about?" she demands, leaning up and exposing her cute little tits.

Jesus, I already feel another twitch *down there*.

"At the auction, we were going to bid on you, just like you asked," Niko explains. "Regardless of the cost."

Her bottom lip begins to tremble. "Are you kidding me? I went through all this for nothing?" She looks like she's not sure whether she should laugh or cry.

Niko's phone rings, interrupting our strange reunion. "Yes? Okay. Be right there." He looks at me.

"Something's up with the missing... cargo. We gotta go."

I nod. "I'll be right there."

When Niko and Vadik pull the door closed, I turn back to Charleigh. There is a lot I want to say. But don't.

"I don't know why you didn't tell me sooner," she says.

"It was a mistake," I agree.

"Am I safe from being sold now?" she asks.

I knew that would come up. "I... I'm not sure. But if I have my way, you'll be safe always."

Her face softens. "Will you tell me more about your girlfriend who died?" she asks.

Holy shit. That came out of fucking left field.

I run a finger along her jawline and down to her breasts. "Someday I'll tell you. But right now I have to get back to work."

I kiss her on the forehead and head for the door, turning back to catch her watching me go.

CHAPTER TWELVE

KIR

Vadik drums his fingers on is desk. *Papa's* old desk. "I'm still pissed. She was looking for a way out all along, even while she smiled in our faces. And sucked our dicks."

"Easy, Vad," Niko said in a quiet warning tone.

I take a seat. Vadik's office has become our default meeting area, even though we each have our own offices. We're used to coming here because this was Papa's office. Why change now?

"Her punishments are over," I say with finality.

Vadik's jaw twitches the tiniest amount. This clue toward his mood would be missed by most people. But not me. He doesn't like being contradicted and this is his way of showing it.

"Says who?" he hisses.

Vadik considers himself an extension of our father, who always had the final word. Which was fine at the time. It was his business, his reputation. With one foot in the old world and one in the new, he had a certain way of doing things.

But times are different now. We are not Papa. We are making changes.

I glance at Niko. If he feels the same way I do, we're in the majority. While the way we brothers operate is hardly a democracy, if this decision comes down to two against one, it will be that much harder for Vadik to get his way.

I never thought I'd see the day when a woman would come between my brothers and me. What the hell has Charleigh done to us?

And what's craziest is that whatever she's done, I'm pretty sure she's done it without even trying.

I stare back at my brother. "*Who* says so? *I* say so, Vad. She's been punished enough. It's time to move forward."

Niko nods in agreement but says nothing. He knows if Vadik feels backed into a corner, he'll come out swinging. Not literally. But he'll dig his heels in just for the sake of it.

Right now, Vadik is holding his pen so tightly, his

knuckles are turning white. He's not done yet. I don't even want to know what he has in mind for her. I'm sure it's not pretty. He's still seething and wants revenge. She hurt his pride.

But he's just going to have to get over that shit.

The only reason to continue to punish Charleigh is to soothe Vadik. His goddamn ego will be the end of him someday.

"If she tries this shit one more goddamn time—"

"*Shut up,* Vadik. Fuck your rage. We have bigger things to worry about. None of this would have happened if Charleigh had known our intentions. I'm not keeping shit from her anymore."

He gets to his feet and leans toward me. "YOU do not decide—"

Pounding my fist on his desk, I jump to my feet too. "Yes, we do, Vadik. You are not Papa. When will you get that through your head? It's the three of us now. You might be oldest, but we all have an equal say in how we do things."

Vadik stares at me like we're having a showdown. After a minute, he returns to his seat and looks around our father's office. I know he misses him. We all do.

Niko, ever the peacemaker, masterfully changes the subject. "The gun shipment has been traced. It was re-routed to Miami and broken into pieces there. We'll never see that stuff again."

Vadik shakes his head. "Fuckers."

Niko leans back in his chair, resigned. "The good news is that this won't happen again. At least it shouldn't. Both the captain of the ship and the folks at the port have been… dealt with."

Vadik looks at him curiously. "Dealt with how?"

The corner of Niko's mouth arcs into a smile. "Let's just say they won't be coming back to work… ever."

Vadik looks satisfied and I feel the same way. The loss of the cargo is a hit, but it happens. All we can do is address the problem and make sure it doesn't happen again.

"What's next on the agenda?" Vadik asks.

My least favorite topic. "Dominika."

He falls back in his chair and rolls his eyes. "Ugh. What has she done now?"

"Word has it she's been a little loose-lipped about Charleigh's escape. It's almost as if she wants to make us look bad."

While that would be a seriously dumbass move, I wouldn't put it past her. She might have a good gig with us here at the club, but she's one huge walking ball of resentment.

"You know, if she's unhappy here, why doesn't she just leave?" Niko asks.

I've thought of that too. "For one, I'm not sure anyone will have her. It's well-known she's difficult, and people think they only reason she lasted here as long as she did was that she was fucking Papa," I say.

Niko's eyes widen. "Shit. Do that many people really know about Papa and her?"

I shrug. "I wouldn't say a lot know. But enough do. Although no one cares. It's her reputation for being a witch that's held her back, kept her black-balled from working for anyone else in the region."

It's her own damn fault. If she wasn't a pain in the ass, I have no doubt someone else would have snapped her up to handle their operations or some such.

"I don't know why we keep her on," Niko says quietly.

You know it's bad if Niko says someone has to go.

Vadik tilts his head. He's getting testy again. "Have some patience. We won't be stuck with her forever."

I think back to the fire. My brothers and I were on a weekend away in Las Vegas, drinking, gambling, and hanging out with beautiful women.

And then the call came.

From Dominika.

How she heard before we were informed, I've never been clear on.

We flew home right away, but Mama and Papa's security wouldn't let us anywhere near the scene.

It's just as well. Who wants to see the charred remains of their parents?

CHAPTER THIRTEEN

Well. I was not in line to be the next Alekseev whore after all.

Too bad they failed to share that information with me before I hit the road.

It might have been nice to know they'd fixed the auction and that I'd not be going home with Dimitri, Alexei, or anybody else.

I'm not sure that what *is* in store for me is a whole lot better, though, because no one will share this information with me either. Which means I have to fill in the blanks.

And what I'm filling in doesn't look so good. Which means I must still look out for myself because no one else is offering to. Any next steps I take, though, will be well thought out and planned down to the smallest detail. The guys are going to be watching me like hawks now and the ease with which I walked out the door in my first escape attempt was an opportunity that is unlikely to present itself again. Not only do they have a new, scarier front door bouncer, but everyone—and I mean *everyone*—in their orbit has been instructed to keep a close watch on me.

It's a wonder I can go to the bathroom alone.

On one level, I am pleased to know, although after the fact, that the guys intended to buy me at their auction. They weren't letting the Alexeis or Dimitris of the world get their dirty mitts on me. That's a good thing, right?

But on the other hand, I don't want to be owned by *them*, the brothers, either. Why the hell would I? I have a life of my own. It might not be much at the moment, consisting mainly of getting up to study every day, working a few hours in Pops's shop, and then heading back home to study more. I had occasional interruptions related to Evie's behavioral issues, but I got to where I was somewhat of a pro at handling them. Although I think her principal, who I have carefully cultivated a relationship with, is getting tired of her shit. I can only ask for favors for so long before the door gets shut in my face.

And Evie is booted from school.

But first things first. I can't help Evie if I'm some sort of freaking prisoner.

Since I'm back at the compound, I assume I still have run of the property. I drag myself out of bed, and my legs nearly buckle from the pain on the flesh of my ass cheeks. It takes me only a nanosecond to remember the whipping I got at the hands of the guys, and when I turn in the bathroom mirror to look at the damage, I am covered with bright pink streaks and puffy welts.

I pat my fingers over the tender flesh but immediately stop. It's as if someone touched a hot iron to my behind. I'm not sure I can even sit.

But there's only one way to find out. I run a tepid bath and lower myself into it until I can float on my back without putting weight on my butt. While the water stings a little at first, it eventually soothes me, at least to the point where I can relax.

I'm pretty sure Kir and Niko aren't as angry with me as they were, but Vadik is a hard nut to crack. He holds onto grudges and never forgives. Of course, are any of them asking for my forgiveness?

Hell no. So fuck them.

I wonder if there will be any backlash from Alexei or Dimitri, not that the guys would concern themselves with those characters. But do I need to watch my back? Will they be coming after me since they were cheated out of their chance to call me their own?

So much to think about. Danger is coming at me from every direction and I have no idea which to fight off first. Or if I even can.

When the guys took me from the pawn shop, I thought I'd be working for them until Pops's debt was paid. And now here I am, only a few weeks later, with what is essentially a price on my head just for being associated with the Alekseevs. To get to the brothers, their rivals have set their sights on me, Kir explained before he left me last night. He said these men will do their best to use me against them. I don't know exactly what that means, but it's not hard to figure out it's something bad. Very bad.

For about the hundredth time, I wonder how my simple little life got turned into such a disaster.

And of course, I wonder when it will go back to normal, although as time passes I am increasingly afraid it will not. There will be a 'new normal,' I suppose, one in which I have little say, and one that will likely be miserable and unhappy.

And yet I have to keep my head up, to continue plowing forward to the extent I can, because my sister needs me. As much as I'd like to throw in the towel and just take whatever comes my way with as much courage as I am able, I can't stop fighting. I won't stop fighting.

Not that the guys need to know that.

Nobody sticks with me. I lost Mother, and Pops pretty much died with her. My older sister left for New York, and now that the Alekseevs are pretending to be on my side, like they really want to protect me, I know better. They're not going to be here for me any more than anybody else has. Yes, they're setting me up to trust them, to believe they'll help me when I need it, all so they can turn me into an 'asset' once again.

Kir might have just fucked me like I'm the last woman on earth, and there were times I looked into his eyes and felt a real connection, but I know better than to read anything further into it. It meant nothing to him, I am sure, and it should mean nothing to me either.

We both wanted to get our rocks off, and we did. Of course, it was that much hotter that his brothers were there, watching me, holding me open. But that's all it was. A diversion.

My escape attempt was stupid. Plain and simple. All I did was endanger other people, including myself. Next time, all impulsivity will be set aside, my escape will be well-planned, and it will include Evie.

Maybe we can drive straight through to New York, to our older sister's. It wouldn't be hard to hide in a place like that, would it, with its millions of people?

But, somehow, I think the Alekseevs always get what they want. And if they want me like I think they do, they'll find me, one way or the other.

CHAPTER FOURTEEN

CHARLEIGH

"Victoria. It's Char."

She gasps, then covers the phone with her hand. But I can still hear her. "Gil, I have a personal call. Be right back."

I hear the pawn shop's front door bell ring, and know Victoria's stepped outside for privacy. Smart. I don't want Pops to know I'm calling her, just like she doesn't want him to know.

"Hey, sweetie. Where did you end up?"

Ugh. For a moment I consider lying to her. If she knows I'm right back where I started, in the clutches of the Alekseevs, will she be disappointed in me? Will she think less of me, having risked her own life to help me, when I turned around and threw away all she'd done?

I reach into the nightstand next to my bed where I've stashed my mother's scarves and finger the silky fabric, waiting for a morsel of calm to wash over me.

"Vic, I'm back at the Alekseev's," I say in a small voice.

The shame I feel for letting her down is crippling. I lie on the bed in my bathrobe, not daring to sit yet because of my sore ass, so roll over to my side, doing my best to suppress a sob.

"I came back, Vic. I came back to them. I knew they'd never stop looking for me, and I have to stick around for Evie, anyway."

While she's silent, taking in my news, I can hear trucks and cars passing on the busy street in front of the shop. I miss that sound, the white noise of traffic that fills the air at my dad's shop, and the sight of busy people with places to go. It used to seem so mundane, so tedious, and yet I'd give anything to have a life that simple back.

It might have been tedious, but it was free.

"Are… are you okay, honey?" she asks.

"I am, Vic. I'm sorry. I've let you down. But I can't leave Evie. I just can't," I whisper.

"You have not let me down, honey, you have to follow your gut. I'm glad you did." Her voice is soothing. It reminds me of my mother's.

If my mother were still alive, would any of this happened? Would Pops have gotten himself into debt? Would Evie be on the bad track that she is?

Would I be here in the Alekseev compound, essentially a prisoner?

I don't think so.

Actually, I am sure *none* of this would be happening.

Oh Mom, why? Why did you leave us?

I've asked myself this question a thousand times over the last ten years. I've tried every way I can think to bargain with God, or the universe, or whoever's in charge of fucking up my life. I've begged until I ached, promising that if I could have five minutes, just five minutes more with my mother, I'd give up everything, even my life. I put out in the universe that if we could only change places—that if she were still alive and I was the one who lost her life—I would accept that. Too many people depended on her. I am expendable.

Mother was not.

And yet, all this praying, appealing, reflecting, and pleading has gone unanswered, time after time. Nobody answers my pleas. When it comes down to it, there *is* nobody to answer them. That's not how life works.

"How's Pops?" I ask.

She sighs. "He is okay. Glad his debts are released, of course," she scoffs. "Otherwise, he's the same. You know what I mean. He's been somewhat comatose since your mother…"

"Yeah. I know. Look, Vic, I have to go. I want to check in on Evie."

"Charleigh, if you need anything, you know I'll help."

I choke back another sob, but my voice cracks anyway. "I know, Vic. Thank you."

I dial Evie, hoping she put the number of my burner phone in her contacts so she knows to answer when I call. But the phone rings and rings until her voicemail picks up.

When she doesn't answer, I text her, a painstaking task with a cheap burner phone. It reminds me of the old days before smartphones, when you had to press the 'two' key three times to get a 'c'. But I finally get a message off to her.

No answer. Still.

I'm not sure whether I should be worried or just chalk this up to normal teenage misbehavior.

Even if she's with her friends, she still usually has her nose glued to her phone. That, and the fact that I told her she might not see me for a while, has me worried

She should know to pick up when I try to contact her.

The whole reason I'm here is because of that kid. And now I can't freaking find her.

CHAPTER FIFTEEN

CHARLEIGH

After lazing around in bed, dozing off and on and fruitlessly worrying about my sister, I figure I might as well venture out of my room and to the kitchen in search of something to eat.

I'm not sure what else I'm supposed to be doing, but if there's some expectation of me, I know the guys will tell me. Until then, I'm pretending to be a lady of leisure in her swanky surroundings. I pull the sash tighter on my oversized fluffy robe, and pad downstairs, barefoot.

If the housekeeper and other staff remember me, they sure don't act like it. As I weave my way through the house, they look up from their duties, nod, and just get back to work.

Fucking weird.

The same happens when I get to the kitchen. The staff bustle about and without even looking directly at me, silently move out of the way as I head for the fridge to see what there is to eat.

"Hello," I say to the cook, who, last time I was here, let me help shell green beans.

He keeps chopping whatever he's chopping, and nods, more at the vegetables before him than me.

Guess I'm *persona non grata* in these parts. Whatever. I'm not here to make friends.

I pull a yogurt and an apple out of the refrigerator and before I close it, add a Diet Coke to my stash. I could grab a seat at the counter in the kitchen where there are a couple stools, but first, my ass still hurts, and second, why hang out with people who act like I don't exist? So, I head out to the Alekseev's parents' garden. I might only be wearing my robe, but who cares. No one will see me except for staff and security.

That's when I run smack into Niko on my way out of the kitchen. Laughing, as we collide he grabs my elbow to keep me upright. The apple tumbles out of my hand with a squishy thump and rolls across the floor. It's quickly picked up by the cook, who hustles to the fridge to get me another.

And of course, because he can, Niko grins down on me with the corner of his mouth delectably crooked up, the usual hank of dark blond hair fallen down over his forehead.

This time, because I don't give a shit, I reach up and fix it.

Yes, I fixed Niko's hair. And the world didn't come to an end.

"Where are you off to?" he asks casually.

Guess he's not worried about my taking off since I'm basically trapped here. And how far would I get in my robe, anyway?

"I was going to have a snack out in the garden. On your parents' bench."

His eyes wide. "Cool. I was just coming in for something to eat. I'll join you. If you don't mind." He looks over his shoulder at me before bending to see what's in the fridge, and I nearly melt.

Dammit.

I'm supposed to hate him. I'm supposed to hate all of them. They've ruined my life. But when I look at this man, the butterflies go wild in my stomach and I can't stop grinning like a teenage dork.

Get it together, girl.

We settle onto the outdoor bench, the cool breeze blowing up my robe. If Niko wasn't with me, I'd go back inside and change, but, like the idiot I am, I don't want to lose a minute with him. So, I sit here and hope I don't start shivering.

"Are those bruises on your knuckles?" I ask, noticing for the first time that his hands are battered, covered in nicks and cuts. What the hell was he doing?

He flexes his fingers as we both look at them. "Yes, those are bruises. And cuts. Got in a fight."

I about fall off the bench. "*You?* You got in a fight? Where?"

He looks away like he'd rather talk about anything else.

Too bad. I want to know what happened.

I take one of his hands and run my finger over a raw knuckle, the scab still forming. "C'mon. Tell me."

He sighs and rolls his shoulders. "A couple nights after you left, my brothers and I went for a drink downtown. Some clown kept bumping into me and I lost my shit."

I look at him. "And…?"

"I took a swing. Turned out he was in just as shitty a mood as I was, so we got into it."

I stifle a laugh, partly because I can't imagine Niko starting a fight, and also because it's so freaking juvenile. This man is a goddamn criminal and carries a gun and he gets into a fistfight with a stranger in a bar?

What is it with men? Or should I say *boys*?

I bite my tongue and press my lips together while

the urge to giggle passes. I don't want to embarrass him further. His face is already covered in mortification at my pressing him for answers. But I am enjoying this in a sick, immature, middle school-ish way.

"Did you... were you in a bad mood because of... me?"

I hold my breath. He could shoot me down here and make me feel like a complete fucking idiot for even considering he was upset over my leaving. Or, he could confess that yes, he was in a bad way because I bailed on him and his brothers.

Either way it doesn't matter. It doesn't change my circumstances.

At least that's what I tell myself.

He finally looks at me. "Yes. I was upset you were gone."

Wow. I don't know if I'm more surprised my leaving affected him that way, or that he admitted it. He *is* the most sensitive of the three brothers, so maybe it's not so strange.

I want to throw my arms around him and thank him for caring. But if he really cared, would I be a goddamn prisoner in his compound, sitting here in a garden dedicated to his dead parents?

"Are you mad at me?" I ask, popping open my soda can. Why I am drinking cold soda when I'm not dressed warmly enough to be outdoors to begin with is beyond me. And yet I just act like everything is normal.

Because absolutely nothing is.

He stares at the plaque with his parents' names on it, and I wonder if he heard me.

"No. I'm not mad. In fact, I kind of admire that you left, and even more so that you came back."

Huh? *Admire?*

"Wh… what?"

He continues staring at his parents' names like he's channeling them or something. "You saw an opportunity to run and you did. That took a lot of balls."

He has no idea.

"And then, when you realized the only way you could really help your sister was by *not* being on the run, you came back, not knowing what kind of reception you'd get from us. I say you're pretty strong."

Didn't expect a compliment from a criminal. They're not exactly examples of upstanding citizenship.

I scoff with a shrug of my shoulders. "It's not like I had any choice, now, is it?"

His jaw twitches the tiniest bit. Did I just say the wrong thing? Because what I said is the truth. I did have to come back. If he thinks I returned because I *wanted* to be here, he's crazy.

"Does… that surprise you, when I say I had no choice?" I ask.

He rubs his eyes, then looks at me. It's funny, his mannerisms are so like his brothers', even though they are related only through their mother. "I… guess I didn't expect you to say that," he says.

"What *did* you expect me to say? I couldn't wait to get back here because I missed you guys so much? Niko, c'mon. I'm being held here against my will. Surely you know that's not what I want."

I'll be damned, but I can see hurt in his eyes. I didn't see that coming.

"I know. I know that," he says. "But you did have a choice in returning. I was thinking you did it because it was better for… everyone." He pauses. "It's dangerous out there for you, you know, now that you're associated with us. There are people who will rape and torture you, just to hurt my brothers and me."

A shiver runs up my spine, and the yogurt I just finished takes a sour turn in my stomach. I knew I shouldn't have eaten that.

"So… you're saying I'm lucky to be here?" I ask.

Jesus. I don't know where my saltiness is coming

from but I'd better knock it off before I say something I regret.

"I don't mean it like that. Not exactly. But in time, you'll know you are protected here. That should be your top priority. Because you aren't any good to anyone, your sister included, if you're… not safe. And at this very moment, you are not."

CHAPTER SIXTEEN

CHARLEIGH

I feel like some sort of debutante.

I suppose I look like one too, with my hair piled high and my poufy, strapless dress. Except what I'm wearing tonight is blood red, not the virginal white girls wear at real 'coming out' parties.

I also have three very handsome escorts, so I'm coming out ahead on that count too.

"Oh my God! I thought you were dead!"

I whip around to face Stacey.

Stacey. Stacey from the dressing room. That's all I can think to call her, since I've never seen her outside it and have no idea what her last name is.

The guys stop too, and when they see me run up to Stacey and clasp her hands, they relax.

"Charleigh, meet us in the lounge, okay?" Niko says with a wink.

Wow. They're giving me a moment.

Well, not exactly. There's still a bodyguard, a new one named Frank assigned to me, watching from the end of the hall. But he is unobtrusive, and while he's no doubt got an eye on me, he politely turns to the side to give me a degree of privacy.

"Dominika told me you were gone!" I cry.

Stacey crinkles her face. "What? Why would she have done that?"

I consider the conversation where I asked Dominika about Stacey, and why she hadn't been around in a while. Now that I think about it, she'd only *implied* Stacey was gone when she gave me her lecture about not getting attached to anyone or making friends in this business.

That woman's such a rotten excuse for a human being.

I shake my head and lower my voice. "Never mind. You know what? I'm pretty sure the old witch was just messing with me."

Tears well in Stacey's eyes, and she tries to wave them off. She's fully made-up, probably about to go onstage. "Well, she was messing with me too, that cunty old bitch," she sniffs. "After my ankle healed and I returned to work and *you* were missing, she said you ran away and would never live to talk about it. I took that as… well, I don't want to say." She steps back to get a full view of me. "My God, look at you. Like some sort of princess."

The contrast between the two of us couldn't be more different, and it has me squirming. Here I am, in an expensive evening gown with tasteful hair and makeup, and Stacey is dressed like, well, a stripper, in her ass-baring thong and spiky platform shoes.

Another example of how life isn't fair. Although she's not being held prisoner, so maybe her situation isn't so bad.

We squeeze each other's hands like lifelong friends. Funny how shared experiences bond you to people.

Now I know why Stacey was off work. "A hurt ankle, huh? That's why you were gone?"

Would it have been that hard for Dominika to just tell me that?

She shakes her head and sniffles. "Yeah. Twisted it. I took a week off. I should have taken two but can't give up the income. My kid has asthma and his medication puts me in the poor house. It's impossible to get ahead," she says resignedly.

Holy crap. I thought I had problems. Just goes to show, there's always someone else who has it worse than you do.

"They don't pay you when you're out? I mean, you get nothing? Absolutely nothing?"

She gives a half-hearted laugh. "Are you kidding? You think Dominika would ever do anything nice for anyone? At least without expecting something substantial in return?"

No shit.

"So she made it sound like I was dead? Surprise, I'm not," I say with an ironic laugh.

"I think she was trying to cover up that you got away. Thought it would make her look bad."

I rummage around in my little evening bag. "Does she know I'm here today?"

Have the guys told her? Or is she in for a big surprise?

Stacey shrugs. "Dunno. But I'd love to see her face when finds you are."

"Here. Take this," I say, thrusting two hundred-dollar bills at Stacey.

Her eyes widen and she extends her hand to take it. But she withdraws it just as quickly. "Oh, I can't."

I shove them at her. "Hide it in the dressing room before you go onstage. It's money I got from serving drinks. Please. Take it."

She looks at the money, now in her hand, and crumples the bills as small as she can. "Thank you, Charleigh. Thank you so much."

From somewhere down a long hallway, Dominika shouts. "Stacey, you're up! Get your ass down here."

Stacey looks at the money and then me. "Will you —" she starts to ask.

I take the wad of bills back and pat her on the shoulder to go. "I'll put in in your locker. Go!" I urge.

I turn to the bodyguard, who is politely half-listening. "Frank, I'm putting this in Stacey's locker. I'll be right out, okay?"

He walks toward me, his massive frame something that would have scared me to death in my 'before' life. "Of course, Miss Gates. I'll wait right outside here."

I rush into the dressing room, knowing the guys are going to start wondering where I am, and flip open the lockers, which are never actually locked.

The rickety old things are mostly full of junk, things left behind by former employees, and stuff just crammed in there because there was nowhere else to put it. But when I find Stacey's locker, with a photo of her little boy on the inside door, I stuff my money into the bottom of her purse. Just when I'm about to hustle out to join the guys, I slam the locker door shut, and the motion causes the one right next to it to fly open.

Good God. You'd think they could do a few

upgrades to the dressing room, with how fancy the rest of the club is.

As I turn to close the locker door that swung open, I realize the coat and purse inside it are Dominika's. I'd know the overwhelming scent of that perfume anywhere.

I pause for a moment to look at her things, seemingly so innocuous without her nearby. That's when I spot a box stuffed into the top shelf that says 'photos.'

I know I shouldn't. I need to mind my damn business. The woman is horrible and I don't want to know any more about her than I already do.

But I lift the lid off the box in spite of myself, since good judgment seems to be a thing I practiced in my previous life, before the Alekseevs got their claws in me.

Even in my heels, the box is a stretch to reach, so I do a little jump to grab it, and of course, because that's how shit works for me, it tips so a slew of photos rains down on my head and onto the floor.

Dammit.

I scramble to gather them together. If Dominika finds me going through her stuff, she'll have my head. Although now that I have Frank as a bodyguard, she might be more inclined to leave me alone.

I don't want to risk it.

As I gather the photos, I stop.

They are all of the Alekseev brothers and two adults who I assume are their parents. The pictures include various combinations of the family—the boys with their mom, then with their dad, and of course all of them together. I guess it's not that unusual for a box of family photos to be in the club. After all, the Alekseevs have owned this business since the brothers were little.

I look closer and find the two older brothers resemble their father. Naturally, Niko does not. I can't tell whether any of them resemble their mother, however, and for good reason.

I have to stare at the photos for a minute because it's so bizarre, but her face has been angrily scratched out in each photo, as if with a paper clip or other sharp point.

Why would Mrs. Alekseev's face be scratched out?

And why would these be in Dominika's locker?

I'm startled by a soft knock on the dressing room door and my heart jumps into my throat. I'm busted.

"Charleigh? You coming?" Frank calls.

I gather the photos as fast as I can but in my haste, they tumble out of my hands and onto the floor again.

"Be right there, Frank, sorry. Just touching up my makeup."

"Let's get a move on then. The guys are looking for you."

"Two seconds," I say, trying to sound casual.

All he has to do is open the door and he'll see me messing around with photos from someone's locker.

I gather the pictures, but I don't have time to put them back in the box. So, I tuck them in the back of one of the unused lockers, already full of junk like old office supplies, and slam the doors to both.

CHAPTER SEVENTEEN

CHARLEIGH

"Sorry, Frank. Took longer than I thought," I said, smiling brightly at him when I open the door.

I follow him to the lounge where the guys wait for me, trying to clear my mind of what I just saw. I need to be 'on' for the guys. They didn't say as much, but I know we're putting on a show, to prove to members that I'm back and couldn't be happier about it.

All bullshit, of course, but I have to believe that if I help the guys, they'll help me at some point, help that will come in the form of support for Evie. I've pretty much given up on myself, of getting my freedom back or making anything of my life, but I won't give up on Evie. And if the guys want any sort of cooperation from me, they will accommodate this.

As Frank and I approach the lounge, I spot Dimitri on his cellphone.

Ugh. Just what I need when my head is already spinning about Dominika's weird photos and whether or not I should mention them to the guys. Hopefully, I can slip past without engaging.

No such luck.

Frank passes through the door before me, and just as I follow him, a hand grips my upper arm and I'm pulled back into the hallway.

"Hey!" I shout.

"She's back," Dimitri says gleefully, pulling me to him so close I smell the cigarettes on his breath.

"Get off—" I yell, twisting myself out of his grip.

But Frank, not surprisingly, is faster. He busts back through the doorway and dives at Dimitri, pulling me free and shoving the man so hard he flies backward and lands on his ass.

Undeterred, Dimitri laughs loudly as he gets right back up. "Our beautiful Charleigh has returned. Rumor has it you took off and the guys had to… you know, put you out of your misery. So to speak." He cackles like he's crazy.

Creep. I follow Frank into the lounge, who still

has not let go of me, I suppose in case someone else wants to grab me.

"I thought he wasn't allowed in here anymore," I whisper.

"Hmph," he grunts. "Something about a request from the *Pakhan*."

Across the room, the guys get to their feet when they see me. But before I head over, I turn to Frank. "Thank you."

He doesn't look at me, but instead surveys the room. Guess that's part of the job. "You're welcome, Miss Gates," he says quietly, without emotion.

Just as I'm taking a seat with the guys, there's a commotion at the door. Because there's always some sort of upset in this crazy world.

A man comes in with Dimitri, and the two head our way. I make a move to stand behind Kir's chair, and out of the corner of my eye I see Vadik slipping his hand inside his suit jacket.

I presume to check the firearm I'm sure he carries. Even in his own club.

None of the guys gets to his feet. Smart power move, when I think about it. To remain seated is an insult. Denies proper respect.

I learn more about this world every day.

But right now, I wish I were anywhere else.

Dimitri is here to cause trouble, no doubt, and as usual, I'm right in the line of fire.

"Who's the guy with Dimitri?" I quietly ask Kir.

"One of the *Pakhan's* men. His number two."

Number two? What does that mean?

Flanking the brothers, Frank takes up position at a respectable distance. The other gentlemen in the club, aside from one who saw what was going on and split, turn toward us with great interest.

"Dimitri," Kir says with a loud sigh, "why you keep coming back where you're not wanted is beyond me."

The insult slides right off his back. "We're here to deliver a message," he says cheerfully.

Vadik takes a deep inhale after a long swig of his whiskey. "*What?*" he snaps, like he's being bothered.

"This woman here," the *Pakhan's* man says, "belongs to Dimitri." He points in my direction.

What? What the fuck? I most certainly do *not* belong to him.

I grip the back of Kir's chair. I am going *nowhere*.

"Hand her over," he adds.

Nobody moves and then, as if on cue, Vadik bursts out laughing. He goes on, long and loud, and everyone around him titters.

Except me. I don't see a damn thing funny about this.

Why in God's name are men fighting over *me*? I'm a nobody. I have nothing to offer. I know some of these guys like the way I look, but is that all that matters to them?

And if it does, why don't they go after all the other pretty girls walking down the street? Why are they so damned obsessed with me?

Oh. Right. It's not really *me*. Not when it comes down to it. It's about power, and Dimitri wants what the Alekseev brothers have. It's that simple. Like children fighting over a toy they don't really want. The fun is in stealing it away. Running over the other kid. Humiliating him.

Now that I've spent time with these men, their motives are blindingly clear. And sometimes even childish if you ask me, which nobody does.

I will say, however, their taste for revenge is *not* the stuff of child's play. I haven't yet seen what happens when someone goes too far, but I have a pretty good idea of what that looks like.

"Fuck. Off," Vadik says, turning back to his brothers like Dimitri's not even there.

Oh God. That's an aggro move if I've ever seen one.

The *Pakhan*'s guy and Dimitri act like they don't notice. "We're not fucking around, Vadik. The *Pakhan* has spoken."

This seems to get Vadik's attention. "I'll take it up with him. Thanks for letting me know." With a wave of his hand, he dismisses them.

Damn. Doubling down.

What are the consequences of defying the *Pakhan?* I make a mental note to ask later.

The man with Dimitri seems resigned, able to acknowledge they've lost the immediate battle. But that doesn't mean they've lost the war, as evidenced by the shit-eating grin on Dimitri's face.

He glares at the brothers, and then turns to me. *Me.* I wish he'd just leave me alone, find something else to fight with the brothers about. Anything. Just not me.

Dimitri's eyes narrow at me and I want to duck down and hide behind Kir's chair. Pretend I'm not here and that none of this is happening.

Just like my ten-year-old self, when my mother was murdered.

But I'm not a kid anymore and need to handle my shit. I hold my chin up, and stare right back. I want him to feel my hate. I want it to burn his insides until he doubles over, knowing that someone finds him so loathsome and detestable. I want to hurt him as much as he's terrorized me, until he cries like a baby and begs for my forgiveness. On his knees.

Someday, I will have the power to make that happen. I'm becoming as hard and hateful as these men. Of course, it was going to rub off on me. It's inevitable.

I know I'm the last person in the world Dimitri is afraid of, but it won't always be that way. Until it is, I will fantasize I have the ability to cause him trepidation, and that I have a way to savagely hurt him.

"This," he says, pointing a finger, "is not over." He narrows his eyes at me and heads for the door with the *Pakhan's* man right on his heels.

I remain behind Kir, doing my best to hide my shaking, when Niko comes to guide me to a chair. He sets a brandy on the small table in the middle, and puts his warm hands on my shoulders as if to offer comfort. I sip the strong liquor and while I don't really like it, as it works its way down my throat, a blanket of warmth runs over me. For a second I think everything will be okay.

But I don't really believe it. I don't believe any of it.

CHAPTER EIGHTEEN

*V*ADIK

There's a soft knock on my office door and I immediately know who it is.

The only person in this building who ever knocks lightly, as if they hope I don't hear them and they can walk away thinking *oh well, I tried,* is Charleigh.

I can't say I'm eager to see her. I know the guys have gotten over her taking off on us, if they were ever pissed to begin with, but I am not like them. I don't know why. It's not like I've had a different life than they have. Hell, Kir is the one who lost his love in a car crash, and Niko's the one who found out our father was not really his.

So what do I have to complain about, for Christ's

sake? When it comes down to it, one might even say I've had it easier than either of my brothers.

If that's the case, why am I such a mean bastard?

I know I come off as cold and uncaring. But maybe I feel more deeply than Kir and Niko. I'm sure some head shrink doctor could get to the bottom of it, but that will never happen because first, I don't really give that much of a shit, and two, I'd never waste my time that way anyway.

So yeah, Charleigh's on my shit list, and I haven't been able to let it go. I'm not proud of that fact, that I let her get under my skin so deeply, in fact, it makes me even madder I care so much. A vicious cycle is what it is. I'm pissed at her for leaving, and even more pissed at her that I'm pissed at her.

Jesus, that sounds ridiculous.

Our effort to bring Charleigh to the club, dressed to the nines to show her off and prove to members that we Alekseevs have shit under control, was somewhat derailed by Dimitri. He's always around, ready to fuck things up. He was like that as a kid and he still is, all these years later. He was the boy we always had to stop the game for because he fell on his face or something, or started up with one of his goddamned asthma attacks. He had and still has an uncanny knack for ruining everything he puts his grimy paws on.

I hear the knock again. Charleigh's still there, and that brings me momentary happiness.

She wants to see me.

For fuck's sake. What is wrong with me? Who cares if she wants to see me or not? It means nothing. It never will. I have no doubt she'd leave again in a moment if the right opportunity presents itself.

Of course, she'll end up dead before she can get far. Our rivals—not limited to Dimitri—would love nothing more than to showcase their prowess by offing a woman they know we want for ourselves.

It's one thing to insult or to hurt a man. But to harm someone's woman is the brashest form of disrespect. It's the most primal way to tell someone they have no power over you and they never will.

When it comes down to it, it's the ultimate act of war. And should Charleigh find herself in a vulnerable spot where we can't protect her, she's screwed. Really, we should just let her take off if she wants to go so badly. She'll meet an untimely end no doubt, and there will be no one around to look after her wayward sister. But the worst of it, for my brothers and me anyway, is that our rivals will have one-upped us in a way there's no coming back from. Nothing would make us look more weak or ineffectual.

If Charleigh goes, it's bad for her, but worse for us.

Jesus, how fucked up does that sound. But hey, no one said Charleigh is anything more than a pawn in our sick and twisted Bratva world. We're just as immoral as she is innocent. It's pure lousy luck that she fell into our clutches. If it wasn't for her loser father practically throwing her at us, she'd still be running around in holey jeans and tattered sneakers, doing what all twenty-year-olds do.

Instead, she's stuck with us sick bastards.

"Come in," I say, a little more gruffly than I probably should.

That's okay. She needs to know where she stands with me. I'm not one to pussy foot around.

My door, or should I say Papa's, opens slowly and Charleigh pokes her head in. "Hey, Vadik. Do you have a moment?"

Being the insufferable prick I am, I sigh loudly and slam some papers down on my desk to let her know these aren't visiting hours.

Although that doesn't mean I'm not curious why she happened by.

She comes in quietly and closes the door, wearing the pretty red dress and heels one of my brothers bought her.

Fuckers are smitten. They barely try to hide it.

She does look lovely, though.

Focus, asshole.

"I wanted to talk to you about a couple things," she says.

It's clear she's nervous, the way she has her hands balled together in front of her waist, but she's fighting it hard, trying to look like she has it together with her chin up and a pleasant smile.

On one hand, it kills me that she's afraid of me. On the other, the sick fuck side of me likes it.

"I want to know what your intentions are for me."

Well, damn. Getting straight to the point.

"Can you elaborate?" I ask, just to be a dick.

She shifts uncomfortably, which makes my cock start to get hard. Damn, I'm a sick motherfucker.

She holds her chin up like she's about to recite a practiced speech. "I'd like to know whether I'm staying here or being auctioned."

I gesture for her to come closer with a toss of my head. She gets to the edge of my desk and stops, barely outside my reach, like she's afraid to come closer.

Because she is. As she should be.

CHAPTER NINETEEN

Vadik

I reach for her. After thinking about it for a moment, she puts her hand in mine—what choice does she have, really?—and lets me draw her closer. I lean back in my desk chair and pull her between my legs.

"Wh… what are you doing?"

I begin to open my belt buckle. I unfasten my trousers and push them and my boxers below my ass, the leather on my chair cold against my flesh.

We both look down at my cock, rock-hard and angry, demanding attention and pointing straight at the beautiful woman before me. As I watch her gaze locked on my erection, I fist myself, stroking from top to bottom. Slowly. Very slowly.

Her lips, now red and full, part the smallest amount, something I'm sure she's not even aware of.

"Pull up your dress," I command.

She snaps out of her trance and after a moment's hesitation, lifts the hem of her dress just until her panty-covered crotch is exposed, a pretty little V at the intersection of her thighs. Now that she's exposed, I swear I am getting a light whiff of her heat, and my God, it's sweet and sultry, like it's designed to bring a man to his knees.

"Touch yourself."

Bunching her dress into one hand, the other hesitatingly goes for her pussy. She presses her index and middle finger between the indentation of her lips, the outline of which is barely noticeable through her panties, and she makes the slightest, sweetest gasp.

"Very nice, pretty girl," I murmur, continuing my own strokes. "Now, kneel."

Confusion washes over her face, and then, leaning on my open thighs, she gets to the floor. I push my ass to the edge of the office chair and point my cock right at her pretty mouth.

She looks up at me and gulps, and it's a miracle I don't come all over her face right then and there. If my life has ever had a moment of pure perfection, this is it. The anticipation of getting one's dick sucked is always exciting, but something about this woman, who has some sort of hold over me I can't begin to understand, is beyond exhilarating.

Get it together, asshole.

She brings her lips to my hard-on, and her eyes fall closed as she rubs them on the precum collected on its cockhead. Her mouth opens and she takes me halfway, sliding me in and out, past her perfect lips.

Fuck if this isn't one of the highlights of my life, to have an angel, an absolute angel on the end of my dick, worshipping it like it's some sort of goddamn treasure. It feels nice, of course, but looks even better.

Here I sit, in my old man's office, head of a mighty empire, with my pants around my ankles and a beautiful girl in a red dress kneeling before me, doing her best to pleasure me with her mouth.

It just doesn't get any fucking better.

And then, there's a sound. I'm not sure what it is, but it's coming from Charleigh. She's not gagging, I'm not that far in her mouth. I hear it again. It almost sounds like she's having trouble breathing.

I carefully push her off my dick and put my hands on either side of her face. "What is it? Are you okay?"

Her eyes are watering, which is not unusual, but then they keep watering, and soon tears are running down her face. Her pretty mouth distorts, widens, and takes on the shape of someone who is deeply, profoundly, sad. Broken. Lost.

Needless to say, that's the end of my erection.

I pull Charleigh to her feet and join her, tugging my trousers back up and putting myself together while trying to figure out what the hell is going on.

"What is it?" I ask. Once I'm dressed again, I put my hands on her shoulders and, holding her at arms' length, try to make sense of her sudden emotion.

But she just hangs her head down, her hair obscuring her face, and she shakes, trying not to make noise, but failing.

What the hell just happened?

I sit and pull her onto my lap, her head buried in my shoulder, soaking me with tears and snot as she shakes in my arms. She's gripping me, holding fistfuls of my suit jacket like she's holding on for dear life and is afraid what might happen should she let go. Her sobs get louder before they subside, and all I can do is pull her tighter and stroke her hair.

I don't know what the fuck happened, and why I'm letting this woman push me to my limits. My usual disregard for anyone other than my family and myself has flown out the damn window, leaving me vulnerable to all level of problems.

I can't let shit like this happen. It's stupid. Dangerous. And will have devastating consequences.

When she finally stills, she blows her nose into the handkerchief I give her, dabs at her eyes, and takes several deep breaths.

She doesn't move from my lap, but she doesn't look at me either.

"Wh… why are you being so nice to me?" she asks quietly.

A dull knife to the heart would feel better than that question.

She thinks I'm an ogre. A cold, heartless bastard who's only out for himself with no regard for who he takes down in his efforts to get ahead.

Why should she think otherwise? What reason have I given her to think I'm a good man?

No wonder she ran off first chance she got. Anybody else would do the same.

I know I'm a jerk. I'm under no delusion I'll ever get a nice guy of the year award. But when treating someone kindly is observed as the exception rather than the rule, even I have to admit something's fucked up.

Not that I'm surprised. I've been left by women

before for this very same reason, for being unloving and disinterested. It hurt my pride. But not enough to change my ways.

I could share this with Charleigh. I won't, though. It's too risky, and the risks I take are carefully measured. I saw what love did to my parents, with their affairs, moving away from each other, and then coming back together. The drama I witnessed, as the oldest kid, convinced me I'd never settle down. Or even fall in love, for that matter.

I wonder if my parents would say it was worth it, were I to ask them right now? After all, they died holding hands.

This woman makes me feel things I don't want to. This is not good for the club, my family, or me.

"That's... quite a question. Look, Charleigh, I have limits as a human being. They are clear. Be a good girl and accept what I can give. Okay?"

Such a fucking lame response. But that's as vulnerable as I go.

"Are... are you still going to sell me?" she asks in a shaking voice.

And here we have it, the depths of this girl's fears. I hadn't realized they were as dark and bottomless as they are.

Dick move, on my part.

"I'm afraid… if I do anything to displease you, you'll cast me off. Like a piece of garbage."

That's when there's a knock on my office door. Not the quiet Charleigh kind, but a loud, demanding, assertive knock, the kind that leaves the knuckles sore but is no doubt heard loud and clear.

CHAPTER TWENTY

*V*ADIK

"*What?*" I holler.

"It's Dominika."

Of course it is.

I take a long inhale and let it out slowly while Charleigh burrows more deeply into my chest, clearly unsettled by the sound of the woman's voice.

I can relate.

Dominika knows better than to just barge in, although I'm sure she'd love nothing more. I have no doubt she listened before knocking, and while she probably didn't hear our entire conversation, she heard us speaking softly. Now, she's dying of curiosity.

Most people who realize others are in an intimate conversation are wise enough to go away. Come back later. Or at least tread lightly. But not Dominika. No, she'll charge in when things are at full-throttle, at their highest pain point, at their worst, just so she can see others suffer. She gets off on that shit.

Crazy bitch.

I don't respond, thinking she'll do the smart thing and take off.

Too much to hope for, I guess.

"Vadik, I'm looking for Charleigh," she says.

Of course she is. And why? Why the fuck is she looking for Charleigh? It's not like we're having her waitress anymore. It's too dangerous. She knows this.

"Dominika, I told you not to worry about her," I call.

I don't know how my father fucked this woman all those years.

"But Vadik, some things have gone... missing from the dressing room, and I want to see if Charleigh knows anything about it."

At this news, Charleigh stiffens in my arms. Then she starts to tremble.

Interesting.

"I'll talk to you about this later, Dominika."

Surely she'll get the hint.

And she does. Her heavy heels *clomp-clomp* with more emphasis than usual down the hallway until I thankfully can't hear them anymore.

Ugh. We're going to have to make a decision about this woman. I'm not one to overthink things—I usually make my decisions quickly and with finality—but Dominika is a bit more complicated.

We've known her nearly all our lives. She was clearly important to Papa, though not important enough to be mentioned in his will. She did keep the club running through the mess Uncle Mikey's neglect created. So, in that regard, my brothers and I feel somewhat obligated toward her.

Which is a shit reason to keep someone around.

"Do you know what Dominika was talking about? Something about the dressing room?" I ask Charleigh, who has straightened up and seems to be getting herself back together.

She looks at me and shrugs. "No idea. I mean, I'm not really working here anymore, so I have no reason to go in there."

"Yes, but have you been in there recently? Tell me the truth."

She plays with the end of her hair, something I've seen her do before. "Well, yes. I went in there the other night just before we had that issue in the lounge with Dimitri."

I nod for her to continue.

"I hope you're not going to be mad, but Stacey is having some money issues related to her sick kid, so I gave her some of the cash I had on me. I stuck it in her purse in the locker because she was about to go onstage."

"You gave Stacey money? Where did you get the money?"

She screws up her face but continues. "I know we're not supposed to keep it, but in the lounge, when cocktailing, the guys sometimes give us tips."

I start say something, but she cuts me off.

"Look, I saved it up, not knowing whether I'd need it. I gave most of it to Evie when I was… on the run. I told her to hide it from our father. God knows he'd be only too happy to take it for himself."

I study her face. Her eyes are wide and I know she's telling me the truth. And while she did break a rule, she had a good reason for doing so.

Christ, she's committed to this kid. Kir told me she comes off as a total brat, but if Charleigh wants to look out for an ungrateful teenager, that's her business.

Family ties. You can't explain them.

"It was my money to give away, and I don't regret it," she says, squaring her shoulders.

In fact, she gets up from my lap and stands in front of me, hands on hips. "Stacey works hard for you. She shouldn't have to scrape to buy medicine for her kid."

Well. If we don't have our own Norma Rae on the premises. Queue the union organizer music.

I don't mind, though. I like that she's taking up for another person, and that given her own situation, she still thinks of others.

Hell, I could learn from that.

"And I never got an answer to my question," she adds, cocking her chin up a little higher.

What can I tell her? That I know I'm a dick, infused with generations of toxic alpha bullshit, where saving face comes above all else? That I can't remember the last time I did something kind for someone, but I can remember the last time I shot someone in the head.

I say none of these things. Because I can't. I can't express my regrets. Because then I will have to do something about them.

"If you need punishment for anything, it will be handled. But I can promise you, we are not selling you, auctioning you, or in any way, shape, or form letting another man, Dimitri included, lay a finger on you."

She laughs shakily. "What about when you get bored of me?" she ventures.

Jesus Christ, this one knows how to push things.

And while I don't say so, because I'm such a prick, the thought of getting bored with her sounds about as likely as my going to the moon.

CHAPTER TWENTY-ONE

I squeeze my eyes shut and am tempted to ask Vadik to repeat himself.

I don't think I could ever hear such good news enough times. In short, I'm off the auction block. The guys are not renting, selling, or giving me away. Now that I've heard it from Vadik, I know it's true.

I want to fall to my knees with relief, but I hold it together. I already lost my shit once today on this guy, right in the middle of giving him a blow job, and I don't want him to change his mind about his promise.

So I try to act all cool and stuff. Which I absolutely am not.

While good news, this does not solve all my problems, not by a long shot. Hell, I'm still essentially a prisoner and I don't know what that means for Pops's debts, but one thing at a time, right?

I'm glad Vadik knows I gave Stacey money. If that's the sort of thing he has an issue with, well, I clearly have a project on my hands.

He listened when I told him the story. And I will bring it up again. There's no reason for a long-time employee who gets hurt on the job to have to go unpaid, especially when she has a sick freaking kid. For as long as I'm here, under the club's roof, if I can accomplish anything aside from keeping myself alive and looking after Evie, this will be something I effect.

My heart skips a little beat. I have a project. It will be a hard one, but if the guys really want to keep me around, they must have taken some sort of liking to me. And if so, that means on some level I may be able to have a certain level of influence over them.

Scary shit though about Dominika and the dressing room. What did she find missing? The photos I found and didn't put back?

For cripe's sake, they were in an old box in her locker, and I hid them in the back of another unused locker. How the hell did she realize they were missing so quickly after I moved them?

Dammit. I planned to sneak back in there at

some point and return them to the box, with her none the wiser.

But maybe this is a sign. Maybe I should tell the guys what I found.

The thought of which makes me uneasy. I'd essentially be pitting them against Dominika, which is not a bad thing because there's no one who wants to see her gone more than me, but that's risky stuff. What if they don't care about the photos? What if they are already aware of them? My ratting her out would come off and petty and vindictive.

Which, to be honest, it is.

Do I want to go down that road?

I decide to keep my finding to myself, at least for the time being. But those photos are bizarre, with Mrs. Alekseev's face scratched out. Like scary messed-up. Not that this place isn't already teeming with messed up stuff.

Did Dominika do it? Scratch that woman's face out? She had the perfect reason to—she wanted the woman's husband.

Besides, who the hell else would do something so whacked?

That aside, I am so happy with the news I'm off the auction block I've forgotten my crying jag of a few minutes earlier. I straddle Vadik's lap right there in his office chair.

"Whoa," he says, catching me.

I throw my arms around his head and he laughs, he actually laughs, something I don't think I've heard him do when it wasn't forced or he was just doing it for show. I rub my fingers over his shaved head, feeling the tiny bit of stubble that pops up several hours after a shave.

I pull back and look at him. "Hey. How did you get your crooked nose?"

As soon as I say the words, I wish I could pull them back in. I'm getting too comfortable with this man, and probably his brothers too. I shouldn't care about his crooked nose or anything else of his. He's not a nice person.

Without answering me, he runs his lips along my jawline, pausing to lay little kisses here and there. It feels so nice, the day's tension slips away.

A notion pops into my head and deflates my excitement several notches. How pathetic am I to be excited I'm not being auctioned?

Yay! You're going to do only the moderately horrible thing to me rather than the majorly horrible thing. No auction but I'm still under lock and key.

Woo-hoo. Open a bottle of champagne.

But I'm a liar if I don't admit Vadik's touch once again leads me away from my moment of painful reality, carrying me to an another where I feel good, and that's all that matters, at least in this moment. I arch to give his lips access to my neck and his hands wander down my back and scoop under my butt cheeks, which he grabs to pull me closer until I am positioned perfectly over his erection.

The one I caused him to lose when I broke down and had my ugly cry.

Jesus.

He's murmuring things in a low growl to me, I'm not even really sure what, but then I'm not absorbing anything other than the way he touches me with his hands and lips anyway. It's like my other senses are closed down to heighten the one remaining, and I'm here for it. Completely.

This is the man I gave my virginity to. Regardless of what direction our lives one day go in, I'll never forget him—whether that's good or bad, I can't say yet.

I want him to do other things to me. Sure, I've experimented with the brothers since I've been here, and certainly done some things for the first time, but I know there's more on the menu to experience.

Vadik reaches under my dress and slides his hands inside my panties to get to my bare ass, and his cool fingers feel good on my healing butt cheeks. I open my eyes to see what he looks like at this moment, and find the day's sun has all but gone down. His office is dimly lit, but it's also beautiful. What's left of the day fills the room with a golden radiance—or are my eyes just playing tricks on me?

Making me think things are better than they actually are?

"Do you like my cock in your mouth?" he asks, getting me out of my head with his dirty, vulgar words.

Like an idiot, I giggle, maybe because I'm embarrassed or taken aback by his forthrightness. "Yes, I do."

His fingers find their way between my pussy lips and he moans lightly. "Yeah, I think you do, baby, because you are so fucking wet. You like my big dick bumping the back of your throat until your eyes water and you can barely breathe, choking on me, don't you?"

His words are heady, leaving my thoughts blurry and disjointed, and there is nothing else, nothing else at this moment in time except my needy pussy, which I grind on his hand to beg for more.

"Damn, pretty girl," he mutters, sliding one and then two fingers inside me.

I hump his fingers and while it doesn't provide the same sensation as his cock, I'm still being fucked and that's all I want. In fact, I grind as hard as I can, chasing an orgasm to wash away the day's pain.

I'm a rutting animal in this man's lap, without a care for the noise I'm making or the mess I'm getting all over his expensive clothes, and when he curls the fingers inside me, my toes curl too and my head bucks.

I'm so close to coming it hurts, so I reach down for my clit. That, coupled with his finger fucking, sends me out of my mind. I am riding the waves of an orgasm unlike any I've ever had as it rocks through me, consuming what little is left of my sanity.

"Hot damn," a deep male voice says from behind me.

I let out a small scream and twist around. I'm still panting and my vision is not completely clear, but I do find Niko seated across the room, kicking back on the leather sofa, one foot crossed over his knee.

I laugh, dropping my head on Vadik's shoulder, and then laugh harder, so hard Vadik has to hold me so I don't fall off him or the chair. When I finally catch my breath, he helps me to a wobbly stand and guides me to an overstuffed chair that I collapse into.

"Where did you come from?" I ask Niko.

He shrugs, smiling that devilish, crooked smile. "I waltzed right in. You two were so busy, you didn't even notice."

Vadik comes out of his washroom, drying his hands. "I need to lock that damn door, don't I?"

His tone consists of its usual gruffness, but there is also a playfulness to it. Something I've not heard before today.

"Well, Niko, I'm glad we could entertain you," I said.

I reach to pull on the little denim jacket I was wearing earlier in the day when it was cooler, and what tumbles out of my pocket but my burner phone.

Oops.

Vadik stops in his tracks, frowning and staring at it like he doesn't know what it is.

But of course he knows what it is. And he's wondering why the hell I have it.

He bends to pick it up. "I don't remember saying you could have a phone," he says grimly.

Shit.

I tell him the truth. Why not? "I picked that up when I was on the run. I don't see what's wrong with having it. It's the only way my sister can get in touch with me." I hold my head up defiantly.

"That sounds reasonable to me—" Niko starts to say.

But he's interrupted by big brother. Of course.

"We have not discussed your communicating without permission."

Holy shit. It's as if the thrilling sexy time I just had with him never happened. What I thought was a tiny bit of softness in his eyes has entirely disappeared, like I'd done something awful, really awful.

An overreaction, if you ask me.

"Look," I say with force, "you all know I look after my sister. That is not going to stop. *Ever.*"

I put emphasis on the last word so they know I'm not fucking around.

"Evie has the number for this phone in case she needs me. It's my only connection to her. And I hope to God you aren't thinking of taking that away from me."

Vadik stares at the phone for a minute and I've crossed my fingers hoping he doesn't fling it across the room and smash it to pieces. It won't be easy to get another one. Although maybe I could ask Stacey…

He gives it back. I immediately stuff it in my pocket before he changes his mind.

"I'd like to go see her too, my sister," I say. I figure I'm on a roll and if he shuts me down, so be it.

He whips around like I asked him for a freaking limb.

"I'll come back, if that's what you are worried about," I add.

"I think that will be fine, Charleigh," Niko says, looking at his brother.

Vadik nods back at him.

Wow. I'm batting a hundred.

I consider if there's anything else I want to ask for, but realize I'd better quit while I'm ahead.

"When you see your sister, take one of us guys, or Frank. You'll need some sort of protection."

Niko reaches into his pocket. "Here. Take my keys. You can borrow my car." He tosses them to me.

My eyes widen at the sight of his keys in the palm of my hand. They are bright and shiny and jingle nicely when I shake them.

These silver pieces of metal are so much more than keys. Sure, they open locks, but the locks they open lead to independence. These keys are freedom. Agency. Self-determination. The kind I thought I might never see again.

Is this a trick? Some sort of mean joke?

Kidding! You're not going anywhere!

I stare at them like they're not real. What if I pick up Evie and just keep driving? We could head to Mexico and once we cross the border, ditch the car and take buses. We could bounce from town to town, stay in cheap motels, and live off street tacos.

Two sisters on the run. We could do odd jobs while we learn Spanish. After a while, maybe we'd even kind of blend in. Make friends. Have fun. Be happy.

Like would be so simple. So utterly simple.

This is the kind of wish I would have conjured a few weeks ago, before the Alekseev brothers showed up in my father's shop. When I believed good prevailed most of the time, and that life had positive things in store for me if I continued to work hard and be a nice person.

How I've changed in such a short time.

There will be no gallivanting around Mexico. There will be no gallivanting anywhere. These guys have connections all over the world. They will find me, wherever I am, faster than I can learn to order a taco in Spanish.

CHAPTER TWENTY-TWO

CHARLEIGH

Victoria has Wednesdays off from the pawn shop, so I head over in Niko's car with Frank in the passenger seat. God, it feels good to drive and even better to be in Niko's sweet ride, a fancy Audi with a great sound system. I'm not sure whether Frank's a babysitter or bodyguard, but either way, he agrees to wait in the car while I talk to Pops with no one else around. I'm hoping that by not announcing myself, I can have a frank conversation with him, and that I might even see Evie.

The bell on the shop door rings and the ghosts of old memories whip past me, whispering unintelligible things in my ears until I force them to leave me alone. I need to focus right now, not be reminded of the life I had pre-Alekseev brothers.

I can ruminate on that some other day.

"Hi Pops."

He looks up from the pawn shop trade magazine he's flipping through on the front counter, and for a second, he looks like he's seeing someone come back from the dead.

From the look on his face, it's seems he never thought he'd see me again. Whether that has burdened him or not, I am about to find out.

"Oh… Ch… Charleigh," he says.

"You're surprised to see me."

He closes the magazine and shuffles his feet, still behind the counter.

But I, being the bigger person, walk up and embrace him. "Good to see you, Pops," I say with a smile.

"Wh… what brings you here?"

Guess being reminded of me is not the thing that is going to make his day.

"I want to check in and say hi. See if Evie's around. I haven't been able to track her down."

Pops continues staring at me with wide eyes, only now he keeps looking out the door too.

"Don't worry, Pops, none of the Alekseev brothers are with me."

He looks out one more time, unsure whether to believe me, and the tightness around his shoulders and neck ease a little.

"Aren't you going to ask me how things are going?" I say.

Ugh. Why did I say that? I haven't come here to taunt the man, tempting as it may be.

"Um… well… hey, I wonder if you could do me a favor?" he asks.

Guess he's not wondering how I am.

And a favor? He's asking *me* for a favor?

"You've already basically *given* me away, Pops. I don't have much more than that to offer."

He opens his mouth to speak but nothing comes out.

"What is it, Pops? What is it you need?"

He looks everywhere but at me. Then his gaze lands on the necklace I'm wearing.

Mother's necklace.

Oops.

He comes out from behind the counter, slowly approaching me. "I… I'm wondering if you can get me some money. Or maybe a line of credit. You know, from the guys."

Oh. My. God.

I'm on the verge of both doubling over laughing and bursting into tears. It's not a good feeling.

"Really, Pops? Are you really asking me for money?" Amazed, I absentmindedly play with the locket.

Double oops.

"And, where did you get that?" he asks, pointing a finger, his lips drawn together tightly.

I tuck it back into my T-shirt and place my hand over where it lies underneath. "It was Mom's. It's mine now."

"You're not supposed to have that. Take it off."

The audacity is mind-boggling. And he must surely know there's no way I am giving up this necklace, the only reminder of my mother that I have, aside from the scarves Victoria set aside. Which he also does not know about.

"It's mine and I will not take it off."

The front door jingles and we are both distracted.

Evie walks in, stopping short when she sees me. "Charleigh," she breathes.

"Yup. It's me. Why haven't you been returning my calls or texts? You know how worried I am about you, don't you?"

Pops looks from one of us to the other, with no idea of what's going on. Of course.

Evie's chin juts out. I know that look. It's her *I'm a badass* face.

So not in the mood.

"Evie, how can I help you if you won't talk to me?" I ask.

She glances at her phone. "I have to be somewhere."

"Where?" I ask. I know I'm taking a risk. She hasn't really had to answer to me—or anyone—since I've been gone. She's a free agent, able to follow whatever teenage whim strikes her fancy at any given moment.

Which is not a good thing, not at all.

She hitches a shoulder. She's up to something. I know it.

"I… I have friends to meet."

I gesture in the direction of the door. "Great. Let me give you a ride. I've borrowed… a friend's car."

She cranes her neck as she looks out the front door. "Um, you know, I'm early to meet my friends. I think I'll just hang here with Pops for a bit." She glances his way and he shrugs like *sure*.

I figure I'll back down a bit before I lose her altogether.

"Fine. I just stopped by to check on everyone." I head toward the door.

"It was, um, good to, um, see you, Charleigh," Pops says with a wave.

The necklace seems to be forgotten. Is the money request too?

I narrow my eyes at Evie. "Sweetie, I'm here for you. You know that, right?"

She scoffs and rolls her eyes. "Yeah, Char. Whatever."

Oh, that I could smack the smug off her face.

Without another word, I leave, heading back to the car where Frank has been surveying our surroundings. It's nice to have someone looking out for me.

"Hope everything went well," he says as I join him.

"You know how family stuff goes," I say, leaving it at that.

Niko's car purrs to life and the drive back to the club is filled with the rock music Frank is streaming through his phone to the car stereo. Niko's car is a dream and while I'm still surprised he loaned it to me, I'm grateful he did. There is something about driving. You're in control. You're moving fast. It feels good, even if it's only for the few minutes it takes to return to the club, where I'm still a prisoner. I'm tempted to swing by home and pick up my book-keeping texts. But I'm afraid that will just make me sadder about the state of my life.

To show the guys I'm worthy of borrowing the car and of their trust, I head straight back even though I also wouldn't mind stopping for a Star-bucks or at the local book shop, like I used to back when my life was normal. My 'freedom' now, such as it is, is tenuous at best, and of course granted at the guys' discretion.

They can take it away as fast as they gave it to me. And I know they will.

I have no plan right now. I'm not sure whether I'm coming or going. But I do know I am being care-ful, very careful. If the opportunity arises where I have to make some quick decisions, I want to be clear headed and ready.

I have to look out for myself. No one else is.

CHAPTER TWENTY-THREE

NIKO

"Holy shit. I haven't seen you in the kitchen in... years."

I actually haven't seen Kir cook anything since Clara died. But I don't say that out loud. I don't need to. It's never far from my mind, how her death nearly killed my brother. Not physically, of course, but emotionally. Spiritually. He's never been the same. Probably never will be, either.

That's how he wants it. Unrelenting punishment is what he believes he deserves.

It's pretty fucked up. All I can do is hope he gets past it someday. So far, it's not looking good.

But to see him in a kitchen again is... encouraging.

"Yeah, well, I'm hungry," he snaps.

I look around. Chef's nowhere in sight.

"Well, buddy, in case you forgot, we have someone to cook for us. So… what are you doing here, and where is Chef?"

He looks at me with narrowed eyes. He's in one of his moods. The one where you just have to leave him alone. But I need answers. This is weird, seeing him cook.

"I sent Chef to the grocery store. There are some ingredients I need."

I lean over his shoulder and take a long whiff. "That shrimp smells amazing."

He grabs chopped garlic off the cutting board next to the stove and tosses some in. He adds a bit of something green, probably parsley, and then a little white wine.

The man is going all out. I'm pretty sure I know why.

"Is this your shrimp and pasta dish?"

"Yeah," he says, gesturing at the boiling pot at the back of the stove.

I lean my back against the kitchen counter next to him, positioning myself so he has to look at me. "Funny. I just happen to know that this is Charleigh's favorite dish."

"I like it too," he grouses.

He drains the pasta over the sink, then transfers

it to a big platter, followed by the shrimp. He carries everything out the kitchen door to the small dining room connected to Papa's old office, where Charleigh and Vadik sit, waiting for lunch.

"Whoa. You made this?" Vadik asks, looking around like Chef might be right behind Kir.

"I did. I've missed cooking."

Charleigh smiles and bounces a little in her seat when she sees what's being served. I watch Kir waiting for her reaction and if I'm not mistaken, his face brightens like a little boy being praised when he gets the desired positive reaction.

Vadik takes each of our plates and serves, just like Papa did when he was alive. Personally, I don't need someone serving me, but Vadik has a thing about doing things the way Papa did. It's an oldest son thing, not to mention an obsession with continuing Papa's legacy.

It's a way to grieve, I suppose, not unlike Kir's avoiding the kitchen for several years after he lost Clara. Everyone has their own approach to dealing with their shit.

How do I deal with mine? I'm not sure, but my brothers have pointed out that since we lost Mama and Papa, I've worked twice as hard as anybody else. Pretty sure it has to do with proving myself to my brothers, that I'm not just here because our mother slept with another man.

Could be a 'youngest son' sort of thing too. These guys were already working in the family business when I was still in freaking Little League. Do they still see me as the annoying kid brother? I don't think so, but I'm not willing to take the chance. I'm going to be at least as successful as these guys and prove I have a place in Papa's empire like they do.

"Oh my God, this is so good," Charleigh moans.

More smiles from Kir. He acts like he's immune to her, but I can see right through him.

I can see right through Vadik too. He's on the fence about Charleigh. It's as clear as day. He's trying to resist her. Not sure he'll be able to.

I know I haven't.

Which is not good.

"Hey, how'd you like the car?" I ask.

Charleigh beams, which makes me smile in return. What is it about her?

Actually, I know. She's different. Pure, clean, unsullied by a life like mine. I want some of that. Her goodness, her light. I need her to brighten my day. Every day. Being around her is like when the sun comes out after a storm. You can't help but marvel at the sky, wondering how its blue ever could have gone missing.

Not sure how things will play out. But there's time.

She reaches into her pocket and tosses me the keys. "Almost forgot to give these back," she laughs. "The car was amazing. I've never driven anything like it. So smooth, and *fast!*"

I shake my finger at her. "I hope you weren't speeding, young lady. We don't need to be attracting attention to ourselves."

She laughs. "Don't worry. Frank was watching the speedometer, big time. He thought I wasn't noticing, but I was."

Our lovely girl likes some speed. Who doesn't?

"And… what was going on at the shop?" Kir asks, serving Charleigh another big helping of lunch.

Jesus, that woman can put away food.

She sets her fork down and looks at her plate, her earlier joy having deflated a bit. "If you can believe it, Pops asked for a favor. He wants money. A line of credit. Something like that. From you guys."

Wow. That man has no freaking boundaries.

"What'd you tell him?" Kir asks.

She presses her lips together and a sadness washes over her face that I would do anything to take away. "I asked him if giving me away wasn't already enough of a favor. Evie walked in before we could discuss it any further. Thank goodness."

"And Evie? What's she up to?"

Charleigh takes a deep breath. "I don't know. But definitely something. I can see it written all over her face. She might be a trouble-making liar, but she's not a very good one."

Everyone laughs lightly, glad to see Charleigh can find a little humor in the dark.

"What do you think she's doing?" I ask.

Charleigh thinks for a moment. "I'm not sure, but she was not that happy to see me and was eager to get away. She said she had to be somewhere but wouldn't tell me where and was cagey about timing. First, she had to go, and when I offered her a ride, she said she didn't need to head out just yet. Like I said, she's not a very good liar."

It's clear there's nothing more important in the world to Charleigh than this kid sister of hers, and while Vadik might prefer we not get involved, I don't see why we shouldn't. We have resources and people. We can help.

"I tell you what," I say, "let me get someone to tail her for a few days. See what we can find out. Should be a very easy assignment, especially if she's not as street smart as she pretends to be."

Charleigh's face brightens. "Oh my God, that would be huge. Thank you!"

I don't elaborate, but there's no end to the

trouble the kid could be getting herself into. I just hope we intervene in time to make sure she hasn't done anything irreversible.

The lunchtime conversation drifts to a recent spate of robberies at one of our liquor stores, and how we are pretty sure it's an inside job.

Shit like this happens in our business all time time. Even if employees start out honest as the day is long, the constant temptation to skim a little cash off the top is impossible for some to resist. At first they think, oh no one will miss a couple twenties. Then, it becomes a couple hundreds, and pretty soon it's a huge fucking pile of money that goes missing, and the dumb ones have actually been known to show up to work in a new car.

Yeah. A liquor store clerk, showing up in a new Corvette.

I'm always glad to get rid of those guys. They're too stupid to live, anyway.

Chef must be back from grocery shopping because he bounds out of the kitchen to take away our dirty plates, smiling ear to ear to see Kir back in the kitchen again.

In another life, my brother would be a restauranteur. But not this one. Our destinies have been, for the most part, predetermined. I feel kind of bad for Kir, when his real passions lie elsewhere, but family duty is not something he could walk away from. If there was ever anything Papa drilled into our heads, it's this. In our world, you're born into your profession. My father was born into his, and even my mother was born into hers, their marriage not much more than a business transaction between *their* fathers.

When it comes down to it, I have no idea what it would be like to have options. Charleigh has options. Well, she did, before we came along.

Something about that leaves me unsettled. It has, pretty much from the beginning. I'm not sure whether it's ever even occurred to my brothers. I don't want to ask. That would be showing way too many of my cards.

After Charleigh gets her latest family drama off her chest, she showers Kir with compliments on lunch. He is keeping his usual straight face, nodding in modest appreciation, but I know him well enough to see he's so happy he could burst, not that he would ever admit that to a soul.

I reach across the table for Charleigh's hand and out of the corners of my eyes, my brothers' eyebrows rise.

Suck it, fellas.

CHAPTER TWENTY-FOUR

*N*IKO

Without a word, I rise and the lovely young Charleigh follows me as I lead her out the door. I don't have to breathe a word of what I want. She knows. And she's going to give it to me.

Another reason to love her.

Shit. I just said *love*.

Outside the dining room, we pass Frank, where he sits in a chair. He is silent and unmoving, and yet I know he's hyper-aware, always scanning for trouble. If he weren't such a large man, he'd be almost invisible, that's how discreet he is.

A great bodyguard is always there, but never obtrusive.

They're hard to find, someone with the judgement to know when to get involved and when to hang back.

I make a mental note to talk to my brothers about giving him a raise.

"Can I excuse myself for a moment? I'd like to freshen up," Charleigh asks with a twinkle in her eye.

I nod at Frank to follow her. "Of course. Meet me at my office then."

I click on my computer monitor while I'm waiting and look over all the cargo shipments I need to track. Actually, we have people handle the day-to-day of all this, but I like to check in to ensure every-thing's on the up-and-up. What I spend the most time on is sourcing the arms that we ship around the world, and negotiating with the people who acquire them. Papa was teaching me this part of the business when he died. He thought I was a good fit because I'm usually level-headed. I can control myself, unlike my brothers.

Hot-headedness doesn't work well in nego-tiations.

Once Papa was gone, well, I had to figure shit out fast. But I did it, and we're moving more 'inventory' than ever.

Papa and his cronies were there on the front lines when the Cold War ended, lucky for them. The former Soviet Union was suddenly drowning in a surplus of arms. Those weapons are now used around the world, due to brokers like my family.

Does it bother me that I'm providing arms to both governments and insurgents who will fight each other to the death?

Not really. If we weren't doing it, someone else would.

Other Bratva factions deal with individuals. One-off sales. We don't bother with the piss-ant street criminal crap. That's not where the money is.

My trance is broken watching Charleigh bounce across my office to look out the window. She's wearing a swingy little dress I bought her and if my eyes aren't deceiving me, nothing under it. Damn if she isn't adorable, probably even more so than when we had her all dolled up a few nights ago. Diving into my work is about the only time I can get my mind off her. It's like everything about her has infused my thoughts—her scent, her laughter, her touch.

And watching her go to town with Vadik the other day? That shit that was hot.

My brothers and I have shared a woman before. It was no big deal. But we haven't shared a woman like Charleigh.

One who I'm pretty sure we all like.

My brothers might be able to force themselves to walk away from her when and if the time comes.

Myself, I'm not so sure.

"Stay where you are, baby," I say, my cock already growing as I cross the room to her.

She looks over her shoulder, her gaze shooting right down to where my trousers are starting to tent, and giggles lightly.

Fuck, all I need to do is get a look at this damn woman and I'm ready to go. What the hell is happening to me?

Rather, what the hell has *already* happened to me?

I'm so screwed.

I walk up behind her and bend her at the waist, placing her hands on the window sill, and slide her dress up to reveal her bare bottom.

"Should we lock the door?" she asks.

I lean to kiss the back of her neck while my hands smooth the perfect skin of her ass. "No, baby. We're good."

She shimmies under me from the brush of my lips, rolling her shoulders in delight and pushing her bottom back against me.

Hell yeah.

I straighten and look down at her, her small waist giving way to a beautiful heart-shaped ass, lightly rocking back and forth.

I marvel at how quickly our beautiful girl has learned—how quickly she's grasped the power of sexual pleasure, both giving and receiving. I wonder if she realizes it was always there for her, waiting in the shadows for the perfect opportunity to be discovered.

I *am* sure she never thought it would be discovered by the three Alekseev brothers.

I push her head down further to raise her backside and part her cheeks for a view of her glistening pink pussy. I have to force myself to take a deep breath and slow down, so strong is the urge to either bury my face or my cock down there.

So. Fucking. Inviting.

CHAPTER TWENTY-FIVE

I swallow hard as Niko's fingers explore, and when they start to slip inside me, I clench, almost coming right there.

That's how sensitive this man has me.

And because I am hungry for release—no, actually greedy for it—I reach for my clit and rub circles the way I do at night when I am alone.

But not for long.

"No," he growls, pulling my hand away and behind my back.

I'm now left with only one hand to balance on the window sill. I'm wobbly already and even more-off balance thanks to Niko's magical fingers.

God, how does he know just how to touch me?

I'm not supposed to like being with this man. I'm

not supposed to like anything about being around the Alekseevs, whether it's the food they serve me, the pretty dresses they give me, or the lush accommodations they provide.

I especially should not like the way they touch me. And yet.

I vacillate between hating myself for this, and just being grateful I'm alive rather than having been auctioned off to some horrible man who doesn't give a damn about me.

How is it I'm grateful to the very men who've taken everything from me. In what world is that fucked-up shit normal?

I beat myself up about this day and night. The only respite I have is when I'm asleep, and moments like right now.

Niko's touch is taking me to a place where everything is beautiful and there are no troubles to deal with. No dead mother, negligent father, or wayward little sister. Where it's just me and my sexual pleasure and endless blue skies that make me smile so hard my cheeks hurt.

I glance over my shoulder, even though I sense Niko wants me to keep my head down. I want to see him. I have to see him. And when I do, a shudder washes over me.

His eyes are dark, focused solely on my pussy, where his free hand slides up and down between my swollen lips.

"How many times have you been fucked?" he asks in a deep and scratchy voice.

A voice I barely recognize.

I quickly turn back to the window and wonder for a moment if anyone in the parking lot can see us. But I know these windows have a dark film on them that lets us look out, and no one see in.

"Um, twice. Just twice," I stammer.

Where is he going with this?

"By my brothers? Are they the only ones?" he asks sharply.

Is this brother thing going to become a problem? It's something I've been wondering about.

"Yes, Niko. Only Vadik and Kir."

I cringe on the inside, wondering what sort of reaction I'm going to get.

After all, don't all guys want to be a woman's first? Like they value our vaginas above all else.

Ugh. No thinking about that right now. I push the depressing thoughts out of my mind. This moment is about *me*.

Fuck everybody else.

My God, how I've changed in a few short weeks.

Never in my life have I ever thought something as selfish as *fuck everybody else.*

Guess it's about time.

"I will be your third, then," Niko says, like it's a done deal.

Which I suppose it is. With the state I'm in right now, it's not like I'm about to say *no, let's wait till later.*

Especially since I want Niko to do things to me. Things I've only ever heard about and maybe even things I've never heard about.

Like pierce my clit.

I googled that and as scary as it sounds, I like the idea of these men marking me in some way.

God, that sounds horrible. And so freaking hot.

"Do you want me?" he asks in a low growl.

I look out the window before me and wonder how he can even ask me this? Isn't it obvious? Hell yes, I want him. I'm not crazy.

What woman wouldn't want this gorgeous hunk of masculinity with his finely chiseled face, strong broad shoulders, and skillful touch?

The zip on the back of my dress slides open. He lets go of the arm he's holding behind me to shimmy the dress off my shoulders, past my hips, and to the floor, where he helps me step out of it. I shiver in the cool room but am quickly warmed by Niko's hands running up and down my back. He takes hold of my waist at the narrowest point, and I swear, his huge mitts nearly circle its entire circumference.

I feel small in his hands, and yet protected. Safe. Sheltered.

One of the few times I have since my mother died.

"Mmmm, so beautiful," he says, feeling every inch of my skin within his reach.

Desire grabs me to the point of being overwhelming. Strangely, tears spring to my eyes and I blink hard, grateful I'm facing away from Niko.

Last thing I want is for him to think I'm some crybaby. Or crazy, like Vadik surely does.

When he releases my hand, I bring it back to my clit. I am aching for him, burning for him, and if he doesn't take care of me soon, I will lose my freaking mind. There's just no keeping my shit together with this man.

Behind me, I hear his suit jacket drop to the floor and the sound of his tie behind pulled from under his collar. A moment later, the tails of his dress shirt whisper over my back before that, too, is thrown to the floor, followed by the clanking of his belt buckle.

"I'm going to be your third cock, baby. Only the third time you've ever been fucked. And I'm going to make sure you never forget it."

Forget Niko? Even if I never see him again after today, I won't forget him.

It's an impossibility.

And then I feel his hard cock bounce against my ass. I don't see it, but I know he's large and heavy, and a drop of precum falls on me.

How I want to see him. Watch him enter me. Slide in and out. Pound me and my hungry pussy.

I reach behind me, unable to wait any longer, and spread my legs as I guide him to my entrance.

"Baby wants it," he says quietly.

His words twist my desire up a notch, if that's even possible. He reaches forward and cups my breasts from behind, and once he's notched at my opening, starts to enter me.

It's a little painful at first, not as much as it was with Vadik, but I am helped by my wetness and the strokes I'm giving my clit.

With a deep breath, I lower my head, looking back between my legs, where I can see Niko's balls between his strong thighs, and I can't believe this is for me. It's all for me. I close my eyes and focus on relaxing, and he slides in with less resistance as I realize the moans filling my ears are coming from me.

Holy shit.

I stretch to accommodate this man, my Niko, and

think if I died in this moment I'd be fulfilled, that's how magical his cock is.

"This cunt, this cunt, this cunt," he snarls.

I wince at his language, but a moment later hold my head up and arch back into him, pleased I can bring him such pleasure.

He slides his cock back out and fills me again with a wicked thrust. "Good girl," he murmurs, pistoning me until I am slamming my fists on the window sill in the throes of an orgasm. It hits me like a tidal wave, tossing and bouncing me through a sea of ecstasy that leaves me wondering why I held on to my virginity for so long.

I know why. I was waiting for these guys.

CHAPTER TWENTY-SIX

Niko helps me to his couch so I can straighten my head out before even considering getting dressed again. When I do, a drop of his cum runs out of my pussy to my thigh, and I press my legs together tightly to make sure it stays out of view.

All I can smell is sex. I smell like it, the room smells like it, and Niko smells like it. Whoever's at the door will immediately know what we've been up to, although it would take an idiot to wonder, given all the noise we just made.

There is a quiet knock on his office door while we're pulling ourselves back together.

Frank opens the door a crack, but doesn't look in. "Excuse me, Charleigh. When you have a chance, Vadik would like to see you."

I catch Niko curling the corner of his mouth into a smile as he returns to his desk after kissing me on the forehead.

"Beautiful girl," he whispers as I leave.

I turn to look at him but say nothing.

He knows.

I knock, then enter Vadik's office. I never really noticed but just coming from Niko's, I see Vadik's is larger and more lavishly furnished.

Must be some kind of oldest brother benefit.

"Sweetheart," he says without thinking.

Surprise washes over his face and he quickly looks away like he said something he'd not meant to.

Strange man.

He pulls a box from his desk, slides it over the polished wood toward me, and turns back to his computer.

Without even looking at me.

"What's this?" I ask, wondering if I'm going to be invited to sit down.

I pick up the box. It's substantial, maybe the size of a brick, and it's wrapped in white paper with a red wax seal on two ends, imprinted with a logo I'm not familiar with. When I move it around, it seems like there's another box inside it.

"Open it," he growls, clicking away on his keyboard.

I feel like I'm keeping him from something and want to offer to come back later. But he did ask me to come by, so I can't be imposing.

"All right." I help myself to a seat opposite his desk.

If he doesn't want me sitting, I have no doubt he'll let me know.

I don't get many gifts so I want to make this one last. Carefully, I peel the wax seal on one end of the white box and unfold the white paper, trying not to tear it. From the corner of my eye, I can see Vadik gazing my way to assess my progress, but he continues to avoid looking directly at me.

When I've peeled off all the white paper, I gasp. The box is bright red and says Cartier.

Cartier.

I know this brand. Well, sort of. My father's shop once took in a Cartier bracelet from a woman desperate for cash. I was there at the time, and Pops told me he'd never had such a piece of jewelry in the shop. He let me try it on and even wear it for a few minutes. But then he locked it up in his glass case. The woman who'd pawned it? She came back the next day, unable to part with her treasure.

Can't say I blame her. It was really beautiful.

And now it looks like I may have my own Cartier treasure.

My heart pounds as I run my fingers over the box's gold lettering. I lift the lid on it, only to reveal another, smaller one with gold filigree. I pull this one out and press a tiny button, popping the lid open, and see a gold bracelet with what looks like screw heads all the way around it.

Just like the bracelet the woman brought to Pops's shop.

I look up at Vadik, who is still pretending to ignore me.

What is going on here? Why is he giving me this? I don't know what it is worth, but I do know it's a lot.

I hold the bracelet between two fingers, itching to put it on, but half wondering if he's going to snap at me *that's not yours, put it back.*

Wouldn't put it past him.

"This is beautiful…" I say, trailing off, hoping he'll join the conversation.

He finally pushes his laptop aside. "Anything else in the box?" he asks.

"Let me check."

I push aside a piece of velvet and move the box around in my hand. Out pops a tiny screwdriver.

He nods at it. "That's how you fasten the bracelet. By opening and closing the screws on each side."

I turn both pieces over in my fingers. "So… you're kind of locked into it?" I ask with a laugh.

He looks at me. Finally. And damn if his gaze doesn't make me quiver. His blue eyes, almost an aquamarine, are cold. And yet, I swear I see a hint of… humanity in them. I don't know what else to call it.

Thank God. Because I was beginning to wonder if he was a heartless monster.

"This… is very generous," I say. "Thank you."

I still want to ask him what the occasion is, but he already looks uncomfortable, like he might crawl out of his skin. So I play it off as casual. Like I get gifts like this every day.

Right.

"Come here," he says, gesturing with his head.

I walk around the side of the desk until I'm right in front of him. He takes the bracelet, opens it into two pieces, and screws it shut on my wrist.

It's amazing. No question about it.

But the 'why' is still lingering. Should I ask? Dare I ask?

"I love it," I say quietly, leaving it at that.

He nods, running his finger over the shiny gold. "Good. I wanted to thank you."

"Me? For… for what?"

He continues to play with the bracelet to avoid

looking at me. "For… helping soothe me. I am less… savage with you around."

Is he kidding? He's still freaking scary if you ask me. But I'll take the win.

I chuckle, propping one of my butt cheeks on his desk. "And here I thought you summoned me because I was in trouble or something. Like maybe you were going to auction or give me away anyway."

He slowly shakes his head. "The *Pakhan* will not be happy, but we intend to keep you for ourselves."

As fucked up as it sounds, my heart soars. Not so much because I want to spend my life imprisoned by the Alekseevs, but at being assured, again, that I will not become the property of some evil man.

Sad state of affairs, my life.

"Are you… concerned about how the *Pakhan* will react?"

Vadik leans back in his chair, hands behind his head. I don't think I've ever seen him so chill. "There may be repercussions," he says. "No. Actually, there *will* be repercussions."

He props his feet up on his desk and stares at his shiny, expensive shoes like he's seeing them but not really seeing them.

"Are you… I mean, do you think you'll regret this decision? The one to, you know, not let Dimitri or whoever have me?" I ask.

He sends a sharp glance my way, like I've asked a stupid question. Which is a good thing. I *want* that to be a stupid question. I *want* the answer to be obvious.

He says nothing, as if he's afraid his reluctant affection will show through.

God, how I'm getting to know these guys. My assumptions might be full of shit, but I don't think so.

"What's that necklace you always wear?" he asks.

I finger Mother's locket like I do a hundred times a day. "It was my mom's. Pops didn't want us to have anything of hers, but I sneaked it out of her dresser before he got rid of all her things. I hid it for years, and when I visited the shop a few days ago, he saw me wearing it. He tried to get me to take it off."

So weird. After all that's gone down with my family, this is what he focuses on?

"He really wanted to erase your mother, didn't he?" Vadik says.

This sends a chill up my spine. "Maybe. I don't know. I never thought of it that way until recently. Do you know something I don't?"

I brace myself. I know he'll give it to me straight, even when it's something I might not like.

"I've... talked to my brothers about this. Of course, we don't know anything specific. But we have our suspicions. Her death might have involved your dad. Have you ever asked him?"

I shake my head. That would come across as an accusation and if he did know something, I doubt he'd be honest about it.

Thinking about that hurts. So I stop.

"The bracelet is nice," I say. "But you really don't have to go around giving me gifts."

Anger—or is it hurt?—cuts across his face.

And what do I do? Double down, like an idiot. I'm testing this man when I know I shouldn't.

"I already know you own me."

Gifts, no matter how nice, will never make that easier.

CHAPTER TWENTY-SEVEN

Goddamn, this woman tries my patience.

I give her a fucking gift, and she suggests, in so many words, that it's pointless for me to do such nice things. I know what she's getting at.

And it pisses me off.

Yeah, my brothers and I want her to stick around. Not because we're forcing her—but because she *wants* to stick around. Voluntarily.

I know she's wondering why I gave her the bracelet—I am trying to curry favor? Win her over with expensive gifts? Show off my money?

She thinks she knows me, knows my type. Rough around the edges and used to getting his way at every turn. That I'm the sort who, with one nice gift, can win the heart of any woman without making any other effort whatsoever. That I can be the biggest bastard in the world and still any woman will spread her legs for me just because I gave her a pretty trinket.

She couldn't be more wrong.

The truth, she will learn, is that we both know things like expensive gifts have no impact on her. I could give her the fucking moon and she'd still look at me evenly and objectively, assessing my imperfections just as fairly as my strengths.

In short, the woman can't be bought, not with any number of expensive gifts, praise, or privileges. She has too much integrity to stray away from thinking for herself and knowing her own mind.

Which is exactly why I want her around.

I haven't met many people like her in my lifetime, men or women, who can judge a situation by looking right through the shiny surface of it.

And yet, she insults me like I'm a fucking blind idiot who can't see what's right in front of his face.

"What's that supposed to mean, that you know I own you?"

She presses her lips together, afraid to say more.

I'll say it for her.

"I don't want to *own* you. I want you here because you want to be here."

She backs up a little, like she's afraid. "But I don't

want to be here. Rather, I don't want to be forced to stay here. I want my freedom. Surely, you know that."

"Then why did you return? Was it just to save your father? And be able to watch over your sister?"

I wouldn't believe that for a second. But I have to ask. Make her say it out loud. I need to hear it.

She scrunches her face. Yeah, she's confused. So am I. Talking about this shit is probably the least comfortable thing I've ever done. I have no roadmap for this. The only relationship I ever saw up close was my parents' and that was about as crazy as they get, full of love and hate in equal measure.

"Yes..." she says.

I look at her, waiting for her to finish.

"I also came back... because I care about you guys."

And there we have it. I know that's not her only reason, but I knew that had to figure into her decision. Without that, it would have been so much easier to take off, disappear, leave it all behind.

"Still doesn't mean I don't want to be free," she says in an almost-whisper.

CHAPTER TWENTY-EIGHT

VADIK

We don't have a lot of what I call 'family dinners' at home, but we always do one on the anniversary of our parents' death. I'm not really sure why or how it got started, or whether we should stick with such a macabre practice, but none of us seems to want to question it. So we don't.

The staff who work for us at the compound start bringing out steaming dishes of our favorite dishes, God bless them. They know full well what this day is, and without a word, they try and make it as special for us as possible.

Hell, they're just happy to be here, healthy and alive.

All the household staff live in cottages on the

property. If they lived in the house with Mama and Papa, they might have died in the fire too.

"What do you think about the bread?" Charleigh asks with a shimmy of her shoulders.

Christ, I love her enthusiasm. She reminds me of a little kid sometimes, and that is so goddamn refreshing. I mean, I think about shit like buying and selling arms and then running the cash through our liquor stores pretty much all day. Profitable as hell, yes, but not a lot of fun.

Charleigh is *fun*.

"I think," I say, taking a chunk of bread out of the basket being passed, "that Charleigh might have made this bread, and that's why she's fishing for compliments."

My brothers help themselves, and Niko moans like it's the best thing he's ever tasted.

"Damn, this is good. Holy shit." He stuffs a whole piece into his mouth and reaches for another, putting on a silly show that has us laughing in seconds.

When everyone settles down, it gets quiet again. Very quiet. Uncharacteristically quiet.

"Okay, guys. Why the silence?" Charleigh finally asks.

Guess she doesn't know.

"It's the anniversary," Kir says simply.

Her eyes widen. "Of… of your parents'… death?"

He nods.

"Shit. I didn't know. I can't believe no one told me," she says.

I shrug. "Figured you knew. Although how you would, I have no idea."

She digs into her meal along with us. "Did you guys live here when it happened? Were you on the premises?"

Before I can say anything, Niko shakes his head sadly. "We had our own places then on the other side of town, and we were away anyway. But if we'd been here, who knows… maybe we would have heard or smelled something. Been able to help."

Kir sets his fork down. This man has experienced too much death for someone his age—first, Clara, and then my parents. "You know, Niko, how unlikely that is. Their part of the house went up so… fast."

He chokes on the last words. I don't blame him. Two years gone is not a lot of time. We're not done grieving. Probably never will be.

Nor will we ever stop trying to prove Dimitri did it.

"How… how did you find out? You know, about… it? When *my* mom… died, Victoria told us," Charleigh says.

"Was she there?" I ask. "Did she witness the... shooting?"

Charleigh shakes her head hard. "Oh no. Mother was at the shop by herself."

Niko looks down at his steak and stops eating for a moment. "Who told us? I can't remember now. The night was such a blur."

"Dominika did," Kir says.

"She did? How was she informed before you were?" I ask.

I shrug. "Guess the household staff wanted a family friend to let us guys know. So they must have called her."

"At the time, Dimitri and Papa were in a heated disagreement. That's why we've always thought he did it. Afterwards, an all-out war was about to erupt. That's when the *Pakhan* came to town. He wanted to keep the peace. Said nobody needed the attention the war would bring to all the local factions," I say.

"So the *Pakhan* is kind of a... negotiator?" Charleigh asks.

Niko laughs. "He's much more than that, but he does spend a lot of time helping straighten out differences. That's why Papa never wanted the job. It's basically thankless. But before he did come on the scene, things were much more openly violent.

So, his arrival was a good thing, when it comes down to it."

Niko snags another piece of Charleigh's bread. Suck-up.

And, of course, she beams at him.

Holy shit. Am I jealous?

What a bitch-ass pussy I'm turning into.

"What was your mom like?" Charleigh asks.

A warm sensation rushes through me. Simply put, our mother was great. Not infallible, but she was a wonderful woman.

"She was into philanthropy. Had a bunch of charities she supported, with Papa's money of course," Kir laughs.

I wonder if Charleigh's mother was anything like ours.

"She kept busy. Helped her with Papa's infidelities," Kir adds. "Well, helped her until she was fed up and went out and committed her own. I think she was just tired of the humiliation and wanted him to know what it felt like."

"And I am the result of that," Niko says, smiling ironically and patting himself on the back.

I go to the liquor cabinet and pull out some port, another habit my father picked up when he arrived in America. He saw people drinking it after dinner and thought it made him more sophisticated. Boom, another port drinker was born.

I pour everyone a small amount, everyone but Charleigh, that is. While I no longer think she abstains from alcohol in order to keep her wits about her around us guys, I can't help but wonder if that plays into her decision to limit her alcohol intake. She typically takes a sip, maybe two of wine during her dinner, and that's it.

Of course, it could be that she just plain doesn't like drinking.

"She was very popular, Mama was. Lots of friends," I say.

That's part of the reason her goddamn funeral took so long. All her friends—and their eligible daughters—came to pay their respects.

And to see if my brothers and I were single, of course.

"She was really social, always smiling and happy. On the outside, anyway. That's how she tried to save face. Everyone knew what Papa was up to and Mama went out of her way to act like she didn't care. Until it was more than she could take," I say.

Fuck, it was hard seeing her go through those times. Part of the reason I suppose I've avoided marriage all this time. I can't repeat what I saw my parents go through. It looked like torture.

And when Mama was fed up, she was *done.* She set out to hurt Papa, to inflict a pain on him he'd never forget. That's how it's done, I remember her telling me when I asked why she didn't just leave. One foot in the new world and one in the old.

And, inexplicably, she said she loved him. Yup, she loved the bastard. It didn't matter what the fuck he did.

"What did your father do when he found out?" Charleigh asks.

My brothers and I all look at each other before Niko answers. I guess it's his story. "He killed him. Papa killed the man. My biological father."

Charleigh's hand flies up to cover her mouth. I know she's not used to hearing us speak so casually about death. I forget that sometimes. When you've been hearing about it all your life, it's easy to remember it's a shock for 'civilians.'

"Do you…?" Charleigh asks.

I know just where she's going with this.

She turns to Niko. "Do you know… who your real father is?"

He looks away. Doesn't like this line of questioning. None of us do.

When she realizes her question is going unanswered, she wisely changes the subject. Well, somewhat, anyway.

"Guys, I found something… strange in the dressing room the other day. I've been waiting for the right time to bring it up." Charleigh looks toward the kitchen to make sure no staff are hanging out, and then cranes her neck to see outside the dining room.

"What is it?" I ask.

"I was, well, I was putting some money in Stacey's purse to help her pay for her sick kid. I had to go through a couple of the lockers before I found hers. The first one I opened, which must have been Dominika's, had a bunch of photos of your family. In a box."

"I'm not sure that's so strange," I say. "Dominika was often at our family events. You know, birthdays, holidays. That sort of thing."

Charleigh takes a deep breath. "Right. I see. But… your mother's face in all the photos was scratched out. Like with the end of a paperclip or something."

Interesting, but I'm still not that surprised, when it comes down to it. Dominika was famously jealous of my mother, unable, for all the years she was with my father, to unseat Mama. She never understood that being Papa's mistress was the end of the line for her. Nothing more would ever come of it. She was a fool to hope otherwise.

Men in Papa's world don't promote their

mistresses. They just look for new ones. And they never have to look far. While such women lack the security of wives, they still live pretty well, better than if they had no one to sponsor them to begin with.

Charleigh shrugs. "I figured you guys might want to know. It seemed like a… strange thing to do."

When it comes to Dominika, nothing surprises me.

"Hey, let's all go to the library," I say as the staff clean the table around us.

Charleigh catches my eye and a naughty smile starts on her face.

Which is exactly what I like about her. I shouldn't, but I do. She's so not right for me. Papa would never approve.

But Papa's not here.

And Charleigh is.

CHAPTER TWENTY-NINE

CHARLEIGH

I look around the dark, cozy library—although not at the heavily crackled leather furniture or animal skin rugs, nor at the beautiful volumes lining the walls, all fancy hardbacks with gold foil along their spines.

Nor do I pay any attention to the oversized black and white lithograph prints clustered on a glossy black wall, displayed as they would be in an art gallery.

Those things, impressive as they may be on another day, hold no interest for me right now.

Something else does.

The three men who've joined me here, each beautiful in his own way, are the sole objects of my attention.

And desire.

Vadik, Kir, and Niko have each taken up residence in oversized club chairs, sated by a good meal, comfortable with their ties loosened and after-dinner drinks in their hands.

"Look at our pretty girl," Kir says, twirling his finger for me to spin around.

I let the guys see me from all angles even though we've been together the better part of the whole day. I shimmy my shoulders and shake my hips, flirtatiously looking back over my shoulder like a coy schoolgirl while I twirl the new bracelet around my wrist.

Sure, I had a conversation earlier with Vadik that I didn't want to be here, but at this moment, there's nowhere else I want to be, crazy as it sounds. This is what sustains me, helps me through my… situation —the admiring attentions of these gorgeous, strong alpha men.

And the way they touch me.

"Baby, why don't you lay back on that soft rug there for me?" Kir asks.

I unzip my platform boots, whip off the white cotton socks under them, and skip over to the rug, taking a seat and spreading the skirt of my full dress around me.

Another dress Niko got for me. Actually, I'm not

sure he shopped for it as much as he had someone *else* make the selection for him. But I'm grateful just the same. It's nice to wear something other than holey jeans and nasty old Converse. I feel pretty in these little dresses Niko buys me.

And I like feeling pretty.

Kir's eyes get heavy and dark, and it's clear that at least for this moment, he's the one in charge. "Show us your panties, pretty girl."

I lean back on my elbows and slowly part my legs, just enough to let him see the crotch of my lacy thong.

"You think I can see that, baby? C'mon," he croons. "Give me a little more."

I do as he asks, and even up the ante by stroking myself, outside my panties, of course, letting my head fall back and moaning lightly.

If these guys want to have some fun, I am here to deliver.

And torment them, too.

Licking his lips, he nods and adjusts himself in his trousers. He's hardly discreet. "More," he says in a low voice.

I pull aside the crotch of my thong and give him a look at what he really wants. From where I lie on the floor, his mouth slackens the smallest bit, but his body tenses when he gets to his feet.

I glance at his brothers and find them watching with interest.

"Touch yourself, pretty girl. Show me how you play with that clit," Kir demands, approaching me.

I drop my head back, and pushing the lace aside, run my fingers through my pussy lips, now puffy and engorged with excitement. I dip one finger inside myself.

Yes, I'm wet. Very wet.

Kir kneels in front of me as I zero in on my clit, and in one swift movement, he tears the thong off me and buries his face between my legs. He starts at the top of my slit and laps me all the way to my ass, which he accesses by lifting my butt off the floor.

Like a starving animal.

And I am so here for it.

As he goes to town on my behind, I return my hand to my clit. The sensation of being worked from both ends is over the top mind-blowing, and I think I could probably come just from this. But Kir is not stopping now.

No way.

He gets to his feet and tears off his tie and jacket, adding his shirt to the pile of clothes on the floor. Next, he kicks off his shoes and socks, followed by trousers and boxers.

There he stands, my hunky man-bun Kir, broad-shouldered and strong, towering over me with a devilish glint in his eye, his erection hanging heavily between us.

I'm ready to spring to my knees and pull him to my mouth. I want to taste him, feel him, smell him. I want him to hit the back of my throat until I cough and gag and laugh and my eyes water.

He has other plans.

He lies back on the rug, and pulls me on top of him, each of my knees on either side of his hips so I'm riding him. I watch his handsome face as he slides his fingers through my pussy again, probably to make sure I'm wet enough to be penetrated, and then he pulls me down on him, impaling me in one swift, brutal motion.

I scream from the sudden invasion, not because it hurts but because it's mind-blowing and intense, shutting off every nerve ending in my body except those in my pussy. I lean forward, my hands on his strong pecs, and dig my fingers into his chest for purchase. This allows me to raise and lower myself on him, which I do with abandon, in between grinding to see how deep I can take him.

While I'm lost in my rutting, I am faintly aware he's directing Vadik to get behind me, and a moment later warm saliva dribbles on my asshole. While I'm still pistoning Kir, Vadik swirls his finger over and around my anus, the sensation driving me wild. I bend to bury my face in Kir's chest and push my behind up in the air. The pressure Vadik's applying lets me know he has more in store for me.

After massaging me back there, he presses a fingertip inside. It's a weird sensation and I'm not sure whether I love it or hate it.

"Try to relax," Kir whispers in my ear. "Relax, my pretty girl," he says, raising his hips to pulse in and out of me.

A moment later I feel more pressure *back there*, and Vadik pushes a second finger in my ass. This time, though, instead of feeling weird, it feels good. Actually, really good. I push back against him a bit, careful not to dislodge the cock in my pussy, and he goes deeper.

"You good, baby?" Kir murmurs.

I just groan. I've forgotten how to speak.

I start to slide on Kir's erection once more, and Vadik matches my rhythm, driving his fingers in and out of my bum at the same pace Kir is fucking me. The crazy sensation that has me near orgasm is not only twice as hot as being fucked in just one hole, but exponentially more powerful. I'm grinding and grinding and there's not a single thought in my brain except how I feel right now, and everything that's ever happened in my past and will happen in my future is of no consequence.

It's like they don't even exist.

I come, and I come, and I come, both Kir and Vadik working me over with precision, the kind of precision men like this understand, my men, the men I think maybe I own rather than the other way around.

CHAPTER THIRTY

CHARLEIGH

Next day I'm at the club again, not because I have any business there, but because I want to snag Niko's car to run over my dad's to pick up my bookkeeping texts. The guys think it's a good idea that I get back to my studies, and that's about all I need to hear to feel like I've won the freaking lottery.

Things are different, for sure, but all is not lost. Not by a long shot.

I hear Stacey, so I poke my head around the hallway corner while Frank gets Niko's keys. "Hey girl!" I call before I even see her.

And when I do, my heart falls. My sweet Stacey, one of the people for whom life is one big, ugly ball of unfairness wears an expression of pure terror on her face, as if for all she's lived through and experienced, nothing has ever been as bad as this moment in her life.

She's in the clutches of the old troll Alexei, who is either oblivious to or ignoring Stacey's pleas for release. His face brightens when he sees me as if to say *ha! I got someone even better than you.*

Rage surges through me and I rush toward them. Before I can speak, however, Dominika appears and her gaze shoots daggers in my direction.

With a grip on Stacey's upper arm, Alexei breaks into a nasty grin.

"Well, if it isn't the prodigal Charleigh. That's what we call girls like you in Russia, girls who think they know better than men."

He smiles evilly, black and missing teeth adding to his monstrosity.

Girls who have agency, I think he means. But I don't correct him. What would be the point?

I smile anyway. "What are you doing? Doesn't Stacey have to… get to work?" I ask hopefully.

Dominika shoulders her way between us. "You have no say in this. Please get on with your day," she spits, her fake-ass smile rancid as usual.

"Charleigh, since you are no longer available, I must choose a new… friend. And Stacey here is lovely and will do quite nicely," Alexei says with exaggerated politeness.

Stacey's face is covered with horror, the likes of which I don't think I've ever seen. I have to help her.

But how?

Dominika stands in front of me, unmovable as a mountain, while Alexei drags my friend away and out of sight.

I'm not ready to be dismissed, at least not yet.

"Dominika—" I start to say.

"You have no power here, despite what you may think," she hisses.

I strain to look beyond her, but Stacey's gone. "Dominika, did you see her? She's scared to death."

Dominika laughs and shrugs. "Part of the job," she says brightly, and turns to go.

But I grab her arm and she stops. I don't know which of us is more surprised I laid a hand on her, but her look tells me to back the fuck off.

"I'm warning you, Charleigh," she says, and yanks out of my grip.

I run to find the guys, any of them, for help, and I collide with Frank. "Where are Vadik, Kir, and Niko? I need them. It's urgent."

"They're out at meetings. What's wrong?" he asks, his face covered with concern.

Shit. Shit, shit, shit.

"It's Stacey. Alexei is taking her somewhere. I don't trust him. And she's terrified."

Resignation replaces the concern on his face. "Oh. Right. He arranged for some time with her, whatever that means. Nothing you can do about it." He turns to walk way.

"But Frank, wait. There must be something we can do."

He hands me Niko's keys. "C'mon. Let's go get your books."

He stops when he realizes I'm not following him out. "Charleigh, there's nothing you can do. Now let's go."

CHAPTER THIRTY-ONE

Pops' apartment is about how I thought I'd find it. In other words, it's a disgusting mess.

Frank follows me in and bless him, he doesn't way a word about the level of nastiness he's surrounded by. He just takes up position next to the front door while I go do my thing. He doesn't even look around. Or if he does, he's damn discreet.

Dirty dishes cover every surface of the kitchen, and the garbage is overflowing. There's a pile of unwashed laundry on the floor in front of the washer and another on top of it. I throw a load in, cramming as much as I can, and start the machine. I have to do something.

On the other hand, how hard is it to run a load of freaking laundry? I know Pops is pretty much useless, but Evie? She can do something to help herself.

And yet.

This is not my battle to fight. I have my own shit going on and if Pops and Evie want to live like slobs, that's their business.

But I wash the dishes in the sink anyway, after I clear the counters and take out two loads of garbage.

Disgusting.

Yes, I have people who do this for me in my new… accommodations, a strange benefit of my even stranger life, but if I didn't, I certainly wouldn't let this shit pile up to the ceiling. I know how to wash a damn dish.

"I'll just be a moment longer, Frank," I say, and he silently nods.

I glance into both Pops' and Evie's bedrooms on the way to mine and don't even stop when I see the state of them. I already took care of their kitchen mess. They can figure out the rest.

But when I get to my own room, which I haven't seen in weeks, it's exactly how I left it. Like a freaking time capsule. I pull a duffel from under my bed and load it with some things I may or may not need, and drop my books into a backpack.

"I'm ready, Frank," I say, minutes later.

He takes the duffel from me, and we head out.

When we get back to the club, I spread my books out in the dressing room, the place where I think I am least likely to be disturbed, and try to pick up where I left off, at the last class I attended before I was taken away by the Alekseevs. Enough time has passed since I last studied that I realize I need to spend some time reviewing. It's a drag, but I'm so happy to be learning again, I don't care. Hours pass and they feel like minutes.

Relishing the safety of my books, I've lost track of time when the door to the dressing room flies open. For a moment, I am annoyed, figuring it's Dominika come by to bother me about something.

But it's Stacey. Or some version of her.

Her face is black and blue and one of her eyes is swollen shut. Blood is trickling out of the corner of her mouth, and she's clutching her shoulder, which looks strangely out of whack compared to her opposite arm. Her knees are cut and bloodied, her panty hose are torn, and she stumbles into my arms.

"Oh God, Stacey," I cry, catching her.

She shrieks, probably because I am touching her someplace painful, and breaks into deep, heart-breaking sobs.

I pull out a chair and help her sink into it as she doubles over and wails.

My own tears are soon to follow. I'm frantic,

trying to think what to do. I hand her my bottle of water, and she takes a sip.

But she throws it right back up.

"W… was it Alexei?" I ask, shaking.

Like I don't already know the answer.

She nods, her pretty face beaten unrecognizable.

Goddammit. Someone will pay for this. I will make sure of it. "I'm taking you to the hospital, Stacey."

She looks up at me with horror. "No, we can't…" she moans, releasing her sore arm.

Her shoulder doesn't even look like a shoulder anymore.

"I have Niko's keys. Don't argue with me. We are going."

I don't tell her how angry I am and how whoever did this will pay. I don't need to.

She knows.

Once she's been admitted and the hospital has promised to call me with any updates, I race back to the club. Frank is with me, of course, but he's silent as always.

I see Vadik's car in the parking lot, so the second I get out of the elevator, I march down to his office and storm in without even knocking.

The three brothers are there, meeting, their faces covered in surprise at my loud interruption.

"What the fuck?" I scream.

I'm not sure I can even get any other words out. I clench my fists and close my eyes so I don't start pounding on any of them, and I press my lips together to force myself to take deep breaths through my nostrils.

"Charleigh, is something wrong?" Vadik scoffs.

Which I am so fucking not in the mood for.

"Stacey is in the hospital. I just took her there."

"Stacey? The stripper?" Kir asks.

Oh my God. They're not even sure who she is.

I hate these men. I hate everything about them.

I narrow my eyes at him. "Alexei beat her so badly she had to be hospitalized. I want you to do something. Right now."

They look at each other, and in my rage, while I could be imagining it, I'm pretty sure they are unconcerned.

Unconcerned?

Over my dead body.

"Dominika knew this would happen and made her go anyway. That could have been *me*. That could have been any girl. But it's Stacey, who works hard for you, to take care of her sick kid at home."

They continue looking at me like I'm a crazy, hysterical woman. Which I suppose I am. Tough fucking shit if they don't like it.

"DO SOMETHING!" I scream at the top of my lungs.

Kir leans forward in his chair. "Now look, Charleigh—" he starts to say.

But I'll hear none of it. These men are callous. They are cruel. They have ugly, indifferent hearts.

And I feel nothing for them.

CHAPTER THIRTY-TWO

KIR

"We weren't here when this happened," I say.

Charleigh glares at me with a level of contempt I didn't know she possessed. Seriously. I'm glad she doesn't have a weapon on her.

Or does she?

"So… you wash your hands of this?" she snaps, stomping back and forth through Vadik's office, an unfamiliar fury pouring off her. "You wash your hands of one of your employees going to the hospital because of a *member of your club?*" she hisses.

This is so much more complex than Charleigh realizes. Not that deeper insights into our business will change her reaction.

She believes in justice. Fairness. Kindness. Decency.

Those things are rarely taken into consideration in our world.

What Charleigh also doesn't understand is that Alexei is not just any member. He receives special… allowances.

I'm not sure how to explain all this to Charleigh, and if I do, will it make a difference?

"How could you let something like this happen? How can you leave that old witch Dominika in charge?" she adds, her voice cracking.

She has Dominika's number, that's for sure.

We're gone for a few hours and things go to shit. I knew this club wasn't worth the trouble it gives us. I don't care if it was Papa's pet project and Vadik is obsessed with carrying on his memory. Our other businesses are much more profitable and far less trouble. We may have to deal with the occasional crook, but we take them out swiftly and quietly and get back to work.

Now we have to deal with crazy old Alexei, a crony of Papa's, as well as the petulant Dominika, who we should have gotten rid of long ago. But it's tricky, navigating relationships that have been in the family for years.

Hell, before I was even born.

If Alexei did take things too far as Charleigh says,

and Dominika enabled him, well, that's something we will address.

Vadik holds his head. He must really feel like shit to be letting everyone know he has another migraine. Usually, he hides it, not wanting anyone to even get a whiff of something that might be perceived as a weakness.

Actually, I think Vadik was feeling poorly before we even made our visit to the *Pakhan* today. He actually let me drive his Maybach. That was a first. He's ridiculous about his car. I could buy the man several Maybachs, and yet he acts like his is irreplaceable.

Papa was exactly the same. Sometimes I wonder if my older brother isn't just a reincarnation of the man. Wouldn't surprise me.

During our meeting with the *Pakhan* today, Vadik hardly spoke. He usually takes the lead—Niko and I let him, since he's the eldest—so I took over. It turns out the missing guns are not a problem just for us. They disturb the entire supply chain that runs through our region and several others.

In other words, it fucked things up for a lot of people.

And while we got to the bottom of who was responsible at the port for 'redirecting' our cargo, and the gentlemen paid dearly, we're still on the hook for the long string of damage it caused. Thus, our visit to the *Pakhan*, where we offered compensation since the cargo went missing under our watch.

Pisses me the fuck off. Another distraction we don't need.

"We need to know more about this," I say, pulling everyone's attention from Vadik and his aching head.

I cross the room and open the office door. "Dominika!" I shout.

Second later, she pops up, smiling and cheery. I have no doubt she was waiting for our summons. She's not an idiot.

"Gentlemen," she says solicitously, looking at each of us for an equal amount of time while acting like Charleigh isn't even in the room.

Vadik discreetly pops a pill, which I know is for his migraine, and nods in my and Niko's direction.

Poor bastard. He can't even speak.

I can see that Niko, always the diplomat, is formulating his words, so I just dive in. "Dominika. What is this about you sending our employee Stacey off with Alexei?"

She smiles and begins to speak like she's been waiting for this question and has practiced her answer. Which I would not put past her.

"As you know, since the auction with Charleigh" — she says *Charleigh* like it's a dirty word— "well, since that auction never happened, even after we talked it up and invited our most important members, Alexei has been looking for… someone to satisfy his… needs." She shrugs helplessly, like she's the victim in all this.

Charleigh looks like she wants to strangle her. "She's in the *hospital*, Dominika," Charleigh hisses. "Thanks to *you*."

Niko holds his hand up for Charleigh to stop. "So, Dominika, you… suggested he take Stacey home?"

She holds her head up. "Why yes, I did. I mean, we had to make reparations somehow. Don't you agree?"

"Did you know he was going to hurt her?" I ask, irritated by her nonchalance.

She shrugs dramatically. "Now how would I know something like that? We all know when a girl leaves the premises with a member, she is out of our hands. We're not babysitters," she says with an eye roll, like we should already know that.

Which, of course, we do. But that doesn't mean members have carte blanche with our girls. Which Dominika also knows.

"You're saying there was no way you could anticipate Alexei's behavior? Even though we know he is a... problematic member?" I continue.

Surely she hasn't forgotten what he did to another of our girls, only a few years ago. The woman was returned to us broken and bleeding after Alexei 'borrowed her.' I wanted to tear his head off, hothead that I am, but Papa was in charge at the time and insisted on handling it himself. All I know is that he had a talk with the man and made some sort of payment to the injured girl.

Not sure if that's fair compensation, but at the time it wasn't up to me.

Alexei wouldn't have done this if Papa were still alive. He was trying to send us a message, like a neighborhood dog who pisses on everyone's lawn to show he's the alpha or some shit.

He's mad he didn't get Charleigh in the auction and is trying every way he can to give us the middle finger.

I wish that fucker would just die.

So, Dominika is not the only one testing our authority, although this comes with the territory. I'm getting tired of it, though. I don't need the distraction. None of us do.

The *Pakhan* warned us this could happen. Our father was an established, esteemed Bratva member, but that authority doesn't automatically transfer to his sons, even though we've been working in the business for years.

Which annoys the shit out of me.

Dominika crosses the room and in a classic bold move, helps herself to a seat on our sofa, settling into the corner as if she were invited.

The sofa where I'm sure she fucked my father many a time.

Charleigh, her lips pressed together and her arms crossed tightly, has had enough. "You are a liar, Dominika. You knew perfectly well what Alexei was going to do with her. He was roughing her up right in front of us," she shouts.

I hold my hands up to get Charleigh to calm down. "Hey. We're taking care of this. Okay?"

Vadik gets to his feet, although I can see the pain in his bloodshot eyes. "If you can't enforce the rules of the club, Dominika, we will be having a conversation about your future here."

Her jaw twitches the smallest amount.

And to ensure she got the message, he reinforces it. "You can be replaced," he says simply.

Her face blanches and she gets to her feet, stiffly walking toward the door.

Vadik's ominous warning is not lost on her.

"I'm sorry," she says without a drop of sincerity.

And then, because she's Dominika, she gives

Charleigh a look that would destroy a lesser woman. But Charleigh pulls herself to her full height, and glares back, narrowing her eyes like an angry snake.

As I glance around the room at my brothers, considering next steps, Charleigh storms out, slamming the door behind her for emphasis and leaving the four of us surprised.

CHAPTER THIRTY-THREE

"What?" Charleigh snaps when I find her in the dressing room later, her head in her hands.

Still pissed off. I like that.

I take a look around the dingy room. I've only ever been in here a couple times, and it was long ago.

The dressing room is a place for ladies only, Dominika always insists.

Another way for her to control things. My brothers and I have clearly given her too much leeway.

Rusty old lockers line one wall, and the long table where Charleigh sits is covered in cigarette burn marks and splotches of old makeup and what I guess is nail polish. There is a rack of clothing on one wall, and an old calendar from several years back that no one ever bothered replacing.

I know Charleigh is steaming mad. Not just at Dominika, but at the whole world. The whole ugly, unfair, cold world. Her anger is good. But she needs to channel it.

"Charleigh," I begin, knowing I should just leave her alone, "I appreciate your bringing this to our attention—"

"No you don't, Kir," she snaps. "You don't give a shit. And if you don't give a shit about a nice person like Stacey, you don't give a shit about me. I might have ended up with that violent bastard. I could be Stacey right now!" she cries, her lower lip quivering.

The thought of Charleigh beaten and battered makes my stomach turn. I know it's not fair to have one standard for her, and another for the other women working here.

But that's the way it is.

She looks down at her hands and lowers her voice. "You didn't listen to me. You talked over me. You disrespected me."

Now we're getting somewhere, and the discomfort is no fucking joke.

The only woman who's ever stood up to me was Clara. I loved her for it.

But I can't fall for Charleigh. I just can't.

And in a moment of anger—I'm not sure if it's with myself or Charleigh—I take her by the wrist and pull her to her feet, backing her up against the dressing room's chipped cinderblock wall.

She resists, although not a strongly as she might, by stiffening in my arms, and looking away, at anything besides my face.

I get it. She's pissed off. Hurt, even.

We're going to address this, right here, right now.

Although not necessarily with words.

I take her chin and while she tries to twist out of my grip, I hold her tightly enough to press my lips to hers, as if that might purge the anger seeping out of her every pore.

It's the only way I know to soothe her.

She scrunches up her lips and tries again to twist away, but I don't let her, and we engage in more of a battle than a kiss.

Which gives me a near-instant erection.

Dammit, what is it with this woman and the effect she has on me?

But a second later I've worn her down and as I hoped she would, she returns my kiss, hungrily, greedily, pausing only for a brief inhale of air, although I'm not sure which she needs more in order to survive. She's fooling herself into thinking *this is sex, nothing more,* but it's so much more, and we both desperately need it.

Like our lives depend on it.

CHAPTER THIRTY-FOUR

I'm angry, so very, very angry about so many things, more things than I can even list, and I'm taking it out on Kir with every inch of my body. I hate everybody and everything, including him and me and the very air I'm breathing.

I want to hurt him. I want to hurt myself. I want to hurt everything around me. I want to cause destruction and pain and unhappiness, the same things that are exploding inside me. I'm tired of bearing them alone, all on my own. I want to spread them so the rest of the world knows what it's like to be me.

As Kir tries to kiss me nicely, I respond by gnashing our teeth and biting his lips and tongue like a temperamental child in the midst of a tantrum.

He does it right back, and it hurts, alerting me that I'm still alive, and that life is nothing more than pain and disappointment and betrayal and anyone who says otherwise is a total fucking idiot.

I pull his man-bun until his hair tumbles out of it and hits his shoulders, giving me fistfuls to grab onto. I pull and tug while our mouths mash together, and when he pushes my hands out of his hair, I claw at his neck, leaving long, red marks where blood slowly seeps to the surface, sure to make a mess out of or even spoil his fancy white dress shirt. I want to ruin everything around me just like the world has ruined me and show everyone I don't care, that I never hoped for anything better because there never was anything better, not for anyone and especially not for me.

When Kir pries my claws off his neck, I close my fists and pound on his rocky chest like I can break him with my bare hands, and in my mind, I am. He's crumbling into little pieces, and a modicum of satisfaction washes over me. I smile through our kiss, if that's what it can even be called, and laugh into his mouth like a crazy woman.

"Goddammit," he says, grabbing my wrists and holding them in one big hand so I can't continue to take my crazy out on him.

And yet I continue to squirm against him,

pressed into the wall as I am, because all the damage I can cause won't come close to how broken I feel.

"It hurts, Kir," I murmur. "It hurts so much, and I want it to go away."

"I know it does, baby," he breathes, running kisses down my neck and behind my ear.

"Make it go away, please, Kir. Will you make it go away?" I beg.

In one swift movement, he releases my wrists and with a hand under my ass sweeps me from my feet over to the makeup table, pushing all sorts of pots and tubes of makeup out of the way with his free arm. When I lie back on the old, dirty table, I turn toward the makeup mirror next to me, surrounded by light bulbs, most of which are burned out. I watch him push my dress up and tear off my panties.

As much as I begged him to do something, anything, I'm not ready for him to fuck me, not yet, and maybe not ever.

But he doesn't seem to care.

I pull my knees together and he pushes them right back open, driving his hips between my thighs, one hand holding me down by the neck and the other fumbling with his pants.

In seconds, his hard cock is pressed against my

opening. I close my eyes, hold my breath, and turn away, waiting for his violation.

It doesn't come.

Thirty seconds later, still nothing. I breathe again.

I open my eyes, turning back to him where he's focused on me, waiting for what, I am not sure.

"Well?" I ask.

A corner of his mouth crooks up and then the other joins it, and in a second he's shaking, trying not to laugh. He fails and bursts out laughing, and as much as I hate to admit it, I join him.

"I'm waiting for *you*, baby," he says, gasping for air.

"You're such a dick!" I yell.

He crooks his head so his ear is turned. "What's that? Baby wants some dick?"

"Oh my God," I say. "Do you need a fucking invitation?"

Still hovering, he presses against my opening but still does not enter me. "Why, yes. I am waiting for an invitation. And if it doesn't come soon, I'll have to pleasure myself all over your stomach."

For Christ's sake. He's got me now. No going back.

So much for my resolve.

"Yes, Kir, please fuck me. Now."

He crooks his ear toward me again. "Please? Did I hear the word please?"

I reach between us and grab his cock, then thrust my hips up until he begins to slide inside. Then, as if I've got him hooked like a fish on a line, he groans and pushes the rest of the way inside me.

Fucking finally. Who knew he was going to make me beg for it?

As he slides in and out, I have to admit I feel better, both physically and emotionally. All that was haunting me only minutes before has not disappeared into thin air, but the wound, the major pain points, have lessened, the sting subsiding from unbearable to a dull ache. It's still there but not as all-consuming.

Thank God. I don't think I could have survived another minute of the agony.

Kir slides in and out, mumbling my name in between grunts, stroking my hair and face, focused solely on me and nothing else. Just as my insides contract and give way to a detonating orgasm, making me feel like pieces of me have splattered on the dressing room's walls and ceiling, Kir pushes inside me one more time. He expands, shudders, and hollers, pumping until I'm delirious and I'm pretty sure he is too.

"Fuck, baby," he murmurs, trying to catch his

breath, "fuck, fuck, fuck. You're incredible. Goddamn, pretty girl."

I close my eyes to savor the moment, to hold on to the feeling that there is some light in the world and in my life, and hope I can conjure this next time I'm looking down into the abyss.

CHAPTER THIRTY-FIVE

Niko

"The... challenge is, Charleigh," Niko says, choosing his words carefully like the diplomat he is, "you... well, our world operates in ways that are unfamiliar to you."

Yeah, no shit.

"I appreciate that, Niko," I say, navigating through traffic on the way from the club to the compound, "but you guys have taken Dominika's word over mine."

He grabs the dashboard as I hit the brakes hard, unused to driving in rush hour. Cripes, if I'm not careful he won't let me drive his car anymore.

A quick glance into the back seat, and I find Frank trying not to laugh at Niko as a nervous passenger.

"Charleigh, it's not that we took her word over yours. We know full well what Dominika did in allowing Alexei to make off with Stacey. It's just that Dominika, at least for now, is integral to the club and we agreed to give her another chance."

Fucking lame, if you ask me.

All the arguing in the world, and God knows I've tried, has not succeeded in getting these guys to budge one little bit on smacking Dominika down with some sort of punishment to make sure she doesn't pull again what she did with Stacey. I take a deep breath to control my rage, and wonder if I can ever accept the fact that when it comes down to it, the guys are complicit. In doing nothing, they are just as much to blame for putting Stacey in the hospital as Alexei and Dominika. I just hope that over time I can get them to see this.

I don't know what else I can do. To make things worse, on top of it all, I'd be lying if I didn't admit this colors my perception of them. How can it not?

"Charleigh, you'll save yourself a lot of anguish if you don't get involved."

So, he wants me to butt out? Not sure that's going to work for me.

I pull into the drive after the big black gate is opened by security. The guards wave at me cordially, accustomed to seeing me come and go since I've been staying there a while, and smirk a little when they realize Niko has let me drive.

Whatever.

"You need to," Niko continues as he walks me to the 'big house,' "remember your place here."

Oh. Right.

My place.

Fat chance of that happening.

"Look, Niko, Stacey is in the hospital. If no one wants to take responsibility, that's one thing. But this is going to cost her and if you guys aren't going to help, I will sell all the clothes you've gotten me, as well as this fancy new Cartier bracelet from Vadik."

Niko looks down at his shoes as we enter the house and nods, and I have my fingers crossed I have shamed him somewhat.

He's not a bad guy, Niko, and in fact, he's the kindest and most sensitive of all the brothers, but he's made it clear he will toe the party line no matter what.

"Fine," I say, shrugging. I head toward my room where I plan to pack up the few things I have of value to see how much money I can raise to support Stacey. The rest of the world can turn their back on her, but I am not going to.

"Hold on," Niko calls. "We fully intend to pay Stacey's medical bills, and I'll make sure she's compensated for her trouble, too. She won't be wanting for anything, Charleigh. I give you my word."

The tension in my shoulders bleeds off a little and I find it easier to breathe. I still might sell some of my things, though, just in case the guys don't come through.

"You know, Charleigh, things are more complex than they seem on the surface."

"Whatever, Niko," I say, and continue toward my room.

But I don't get far before he grabs my upper arm.

"You need to stop this," he says quietly.

And just like that, I am reminded of my place here with the Alekseev family, the place I fell into thanks to my father's careless ways.

"I'm making a point here," he says.

"And what's that?" I ask.

"Dominika is… Dominika is a relative of mine."

"*What?*" I ask quietly.

"She's… she's my aunt. Her brother was my father."

CHAPTER THIRTY-SIX

No one outside the family knows our secret.

It's bad enough I don't have the same father as Vadik and Kir, but the fact that I'm related to the psycho Dominika is a secret I hope to take to my grave.

Dominika knows, of course. She also knows to refrain from bringing it up. But it's always there, hanging in front of my face like a piece of smelly, rotten meat.

That I could be related to someone I basically detest is not a good feeling. It's bad enough being the byproduct of the affair of a woman desperate to give her philandering husband a taste of his own medicine. But that my mother went after Dominika's brother, an act she knew would crucify the heart of her husband, was about the coldest, cruelest thing she could do.

She got her message across. Grigory Alekseev, as I understand it, promptly shot my real father in the head and adopted me, before word could ever get out there was trouble on the home front. Of course, I didn't know any of this until I got older.

But my mother flexed her muscle the only way she knew how, and afterward, her husband came home to her a lot more often. Not every night—the man was not transformed into an angel—but he cut back on his dalliances for the sake of his family.

My parents did love each other. Of that, I've always been sure, even when I learned about the dark sides of their relationship. They were a product of the old world, and the way they did things was the way they were taught. A more modern woman might have packed her kids, her bags, and left. But that wasn't an option for Mama, who did what she could.

"Are you shitting me?" Charleigh asks, her face pale when I share my secret. "You are *related* to that woman?"

I release a small laugh, anything but amused by the subject. "Yup. It's true. Mama had an affair with Dominika's brother to stick it to Papa. Hardly anyone knows. But I wanted you to. It might help you… understand some of the things you deal with around here. Our world is not… typical."

Charleigh grabs the banister as she heads upstairs, as if she needs to steady herself. "Yeah. I'm getting that picture," she says, shaking her head slowly. "Do you think… that has anything to do with why those weird pictures were in her locker? Of your family with your mom scratched out?"

I shrug. Who the fuck knows. Crazy town has been my life for as long as I can remember. I stopped trying to make sense out of it a long time ago.

"Any other bombs you want to drop on me?" she asks.

"That's enough for today."

"Okay. Well thanks for sharing that interesting tidbit. I'm going to my room now, unless you want some *servicing*?"

Servicing? What the fuck?

Without an answer, I turn on my heel and head for the library for a drink. At this moment, I don't give a shit what Charleigh does.

Pain in the ass.

Servicing. Nice.

Brings me back to when Papa decided it was time for me to lose my virginity. He told Mama he was taking me *out*. She asked no questions. I am sure she knew.

We arrived at a brothel of sorts and while I was scared shitless, I held my head up just like Papa did, smiling broadly like I belonged there, knew what to do, and was capable of 'taking care of business.'

It wasn't a horrible experience, nor was it particularly pleasant. The woman Papa selected for me seemed barely older than myself, and when the door was closed and we had our clothes off, was nearly as inexperienced. We made small talk, kissed, and fumbled until I got my condom on and awkwardly entered her. It was over, from start to finish, in fifteen minutes. When I returned to the lounge after my *service*, Papa was waiting for me with a drink in his hand, chatting with the proprietor.

I knew by the way he looked at me he was surprised how quickly I returned. But because he'd just been poured his favorite scotch, he wasn't about to leave, as much as I was dying to. He sipped his drink and enjoyed chatting with all the ladies while I slumped in a chair in the corner, trying to ignore the whispers, giggles, and pointing as word spread that I was a first-timer.

In short, it was a shitty experience.

So, Charleigh's comment about *servicing* me didn't sit well. The difference is that it's ten years later, I'm drinking my own damn whiskey, and I don't put up with shit from anyone.

Drink in hand, I bound up the stairs two at a time toward Charleigh's room, wondering if she's happy she managed to throw a bit of her shit mood my way.

I barge in without knocking, startling the hell out of her, and storm across the room with such fury she backs herself up against the wall.

"What… what are you doing? Niko? What's going on?" she stumbles.

Anger seeps out of my pores as I set my drink down and open my trousers. "You were right earlier, on the stairs. You are going to service me."

I whip out my erection, hard and angry just like I am and put a hand on Charleigh's shoulder in case she's not sure what to do next.

"I… I…" she stutters.

But she silences when she gets to her knees and I brush the wet head of my cock against her cheek. In spite of herself, her eyes get heavy and she rubs against me like a cat on someone's leg.

I take her by the chin and push past her lips until I hit the back of her throat and she gags. I pull back out and she gasps, coughing and catching her breath, and I drive into her mouth again. She finally finds a rhythm and takes a hold of the root of my dick and my balls with her other hand, and starts sucking the life out of me.

I lean on the wall over her head and rock in and out of her wet mouth, expertly getting me off. And if I'm not mistaken, she's even moaning quietly as she picks up the pace. In moments, my balls throb and a pressure builds at my base, and then I'm coming down Charleigh's throat.

And goddamn if she isn't swallowing everything I'm giving her.

When I'm done, I pull out and Charleigh pulls herself to her feet, looking at me with narrowed, contemptuous eyes. "Happy now?"

Fuck all, she's not giving in.

"It was okay," I say, shrugging.

She snickers. "That's good, because it was only supposed to be okay."

I walk to her bathroom for a towel and when I come back into the room, I toss it in her direction.

While the orgasm was nice—when isn't an orgasm nice?—it was cold and impersonal, exactly what Charleigh intended.

She takes a seat on the edge of her bed. "I appreciate your sharing your secret with me," she says without looking at me.

Are we getting somewhere?

"And I'm sorry you're related to that horrible woman," she adds.

Yeah. Me too.

"Sorry I lashed out like I did," I say. "If I'd been at the club the day Alexei took Stacey, I would have stopped him."

Charleigh nods. "I think I know why Dominika let it happen. I think it was her basically giving me the middle finger. She knew how much it would bother me, and how it would drive a wedge between you guys and me."

I wouldn't put it past Dominika to be so calculating. But talk about biting the hand that feeds you.

Crazy bitch.

Having established some sort of truce, at least in my mind, there is still a chill between Charleigh and me. It might take a while to thaw.

Or, it might never.

I want Charleigh to stay, but I want her to *want* to. And if she does, that means she needs to learn to coexist with Dominika.

Not sure I see that happening. But when push comes to shove, if it's between the two women, well, there's not even a need for a conversation to be had. Dominika, whether she's my aunt or not, will be gone.

I know I shouldn't look at it this way. My top priority should be keeping Papa's legacy alive by making sure his businesses thrive. Not falling in love with the lovely Charleigh.

I've got to get this woman out of my head but I just don't know how. When I'm with her, I can't stop looking at her, and when we're apart, I can't stop thinking about her. This is fucking with my head.

And I'm afraid it's too late to do anything about it.

CHAPTER THIRTY-SEVEN

NIKO

"Dominika, may I have a moment?"

She stops in her tracks and slowly turns, like my request is a bother.

God, she's a bitch.

I hold my office door open so she knows I'm waiting.

"What can I do for you, Niko?" she asks, her eyes twinkling.

If she thinks she has some sort of advantage here because we're related, she couldn't be more off-base.

"I have been told there were a bunch of photos in the dressing room, photos of my family, with my mother's face scratched out, in somebody's locker. What do you know about this?"

I don't want to say too much, although she'll

probably guess I got my information from Charleigh.

She looks at me, expressionless, as she decides which bullshit lie she wants to lay on me.

Why am I even bothering?

Of course, I never thought for a moment she was going to be real with me, but I do want to see how she reacts. That will tell me most everything I need to know.

"I don't know what you're talking about," she says, her eyes wide.

It's all I can do to keep from bursting out laughing, that's how predictable her answer is. But it's just a starting point.

"Were you storing photos of my family in the locker room?"

She sidles up to me like we're buddies, and when I take a step back for some space, a darkness washes over her face at the insult.

Tough shit.

"I've been part of your family since before you were born, Niko. I've been there for every baptism, holiday, vacation, graduation, you name it. Would it really strike you as odd if I did have some photos to remember all the happy times we all had together?"

"So you're saying you *do* have photos. And I guess

you crossed my mother's face out because of the... issues between the two of you?"

She pulls her shoulders back and stretches to her full height, which, with the skyscraper shoes she wears, nearly puts her on eye level with my six-foot-three inches. As she takes another step closer, which I really don't appreciate, I can see the creases in her face where the day's makeup has already settled.

Papa, how did you...

Never mind.

She shrugs with nonchalance. "So what if I have some Alekseev family photos in my things? First, I have every right to, second, I'd like to know who was going through my things, and third, what are you going to do about it?"

This woman has no idea how thin the ice she's skating on is. I could drag her sorry ass out the front door and tell her never to come back if I wanted.

And someday I will.

But today is not that day.

I force my fingers, balled into tight fists, to relax. The last thing I want is for Dominika to know she's getting under my skin. That if I had my choice, I'd put my fingers around her neck right here, right now, and squeeze the undeserving life out of her.

Fuck all, I sound like one of my brothers, always ready to strike first and ask questions later.

Get your shit together, asshole.

"Are you going to answer these questions for me… my favorite nephew?" she croons.

She's pulling out the big guns. I can count on one hand the number of times this, our being related, has come up in conversation over the years. Papa forbade anyone to talk about it so word wouldn't get out, not so much that he took in another man's son, but that his wife had the nerve to step out on him.

Never mind that for men like him, female 'companionship' outside marriage is a foregone conclusion.

Double standards, yo.

I cross my office and hold open the door to signal to Dominika that I'm done with her.

She smiles as she slinks past. "You know, Niko, your father would not approve."

I frown at her. "Of what? Of what would he not approve?"

She tilts her head and the smug seeps out of her pores. "Charleigh. Your father would never approve of Charleigh."

And there we have it.

Of course that's what's on her mind. She hasn't approved of Charleigh since the day she arrived. I'm not surprised at her sentiments—she never did much to hide them. But her voicing them out loud is a step too far.

"If my father were here today, Dominika, I don't think he'd be very happy you feel you have the right to speak for him. About anything."

She sniffs and walks out the door, but not before turning back, hands on her hips. "She's not from our world, Niko. She'll just make trouble for you, your brothers, for all of us. I see all of you, falling for her quiet beauty. She's different from the other girls you know. Sweet, innocent. Not a mean bone in her body. But she's not the kind of woman you need—"

I start to close my office door. I've heard enough.

But Dominika's arm shoots out faster than I can, and she stops the door. "Niko, your parents are gone. Someone has to look out for you and your brothers. I'm telling you, don't fall for that woman. Don't fall for her any further than you already have."

CHAPTER THIRTY-EIGHT

Text books back in my possession, I feel like a new woman. Because I don't have much else to fill my days with, I've gone back to the beginning of each book, studying harder than I did the first time around. If I ever get to be a bookkeeper, I'll be a damn good one.

I'm picking through a chapter that on the first go-round, I found challenging, but now that I can take my time, it's really coming together.

There's a knock on my bedroom door.

"Come in," I call, keeping my voice flat and disinterested.

I'm still not sure how I feel about the guys since Stacey was beaten by Alexei. I want that to come across loud and clear, like I'm still upset with them.

Which I am.

But if that's the case, how come every time I see one of them, my heart skips a beat?

"Hey," Niko says, poking his head into my room. "Do you have a moment?"

I close my book and set it aside on the bed where I'm studying. It's funny, I have this huge room with a desk and comfortable chairs, and where do I study? On the bed.

I've always studied in bed, for as long as I can remember. Habits are comforting, and if I've learned anything in recent weeks, it's to grab comfort where I can.

"Since you got your books, I feel like we hardly see you," Niko says, taking a seat on the edge of my bed.

I shrug like I don't care. I can't let anyone know how much my books and studies mean to me. They'll use them against me. Turn them into a weapon. Hurt me by taking away one of the few pleasures I have.

"It's good to be back to the books. I've missed them," I say casually, tossing my pencil in the air.

I'm struggling to hold onto the anger that has fueled me these past few days. It's given me courage —the courage to stand up to Dominika, to express my upset with the guys, to dive back into my books after falling behind—it's like I was a sputtering little flame that someone poured gasoline on.

I feel unstoppable now. I might not be, but I feel like it.

Niko reaches into his suit coat pocket and pulls out a folded envelope. "Got something here for you." He tosses it across the bed to me.

I pick it up and when I open it, find there are photos inside.

Photos of my little sister, Evie.

"What… where did you get these? What is Evie doing with these people?" I stammer, trying to swallow away the bad taste in the back of my throat.

I knew Niko had someone tail Evie, but I thought she'd just be hanging out with her girlfriends, sneaking a smoke, or maybe even shoplifting again like little idiots.

But these aren't her school friends in the photos. I don't know who these people are. And I don't recognize anything about where she is. In one photo, there is a boy about her age with his arm slung around her. She's looking up at him with a smile, and he's looking down at her, doing the same.

I know that look on her face because I've had that look on mine. She likes the boy. She has a crush on him. She's susceptible to things he might ask of her.

Which would be fine for a kid like me, who was

shy and serious and could never be talked into doing anything I didn't want to.

Evie is not like that. Evie is impressionable, desperate to be liked, and hungry for the attention of males.

"I... I don't know who this boy is. I didn't even know she... liked a boy."

Is he her boyfriend? Is he nice to her? Does he treat her well?

And what the hell is his name?

Niko continues. "I don't have a good feeling about this, Charleigh. First of all, she's hanging out in an arcade where there are a lot of undesirable types."

Oh God. "What do you mean? Drugs and so forth?"

He nods. "There's that, yes, but also gang activity and lots of young punks trying to prove how cool they are."

"Does that mean—"

I can't continue my thought.

I don't have to. Niko gets it. "Yes. Just like the boys have to show their toughness, the girls have to do... some things too. They're not good people, Charleigh."

It's ironic for Niko to talk to me about who are and are not 'good people,' but I get his point. You don't want a sixteen-year-old kid who's already known for making poor choices around kids looking for trouble.

My father is probably completely unaware. Hell, Evie could never come home again and I'm not sure Pops would even notice.

"Who... who is the boy? Do you know? Is he from her school?"

While Evie might be hanging out with trouble-makers, knowing they're from her school will give me a modicum of comfort. I'm not sure why, but it somehow makes the whole situation seem more manageable.

"Don't you recognize him?" Niko asks.

"What?" I pull the photo closer and study the boy. I can only see him in profile while he gazes down at my sister.

I have no idea who he is.

I stop. I don't like the way Niko is looking at me.

"What?" I demand. "Who is he, Niko?"

"We're not sure. But we're trying to find out. We think he might be someone hired by Dimitri. He may be his nephew."

My hands fly to my mouth because I'm sure I'm about to vomit. My eyes fill with tears, and the room spins around me.

Oh God no. Please. Just, no.

I clutch my silver locket. Mother, if you're out there, this is the time I need you.

What is my sister doing hanging out with a relative of Dimitri's?

I jump off my bed and run for my sneakers. "I've got to go to her right now, Niko. Take me to her. Please."

But he stays seated on my bed. As in he's not getting up. He's not going to help me get to Evie.

So I decide to force him. I race back across the room and grab him by the arm, yanking as hard as I can. If he's not getting up off his ass by himself, I will make him.

And while I'm pulling with all the force I can, he barely budges.

Because of course.

"Niko, come on," I beg, my voice starting to break.

He pries my hand off and holds it. "Wait a minute, Charleigh. This is not how it's done. We don't just show up there and drag Evie out. Do you realize how that could backfire?"

Backfire? I don't give a shit about any backfire. I want my sister out of the clutches of those people.

"Niko, please—"

He shakes his head.

So I run for my phone and call Evie. I have no idea what I will say.

How will she react when she finds out I had someone follow her?

"Charleigh, hold on, for Christ's sake," Niko yells, startling me.

My hands are shaking, the adrenaline is running so hard. My thoughts are scattered and make no sense.

I'm panicking and don't know what to do.

Niko pats the bed next to him. "C'mon. Sit down for a moment. Let's talk this through. I know you're upset and I don't blame you. But if we barge in, it will just serve to push your sister deeper into their world. We have to be careful how we go about getting her out."

Okay. That makes sense. Like a cult or something.

"How long, Niko? How long will it take? Oh God, what if Dimitri gets his hands on her?" I'm panicking again, moments from getting sick, and unable to run for the bathroom because I'm shaking so hard.

"I don't know, but we'll move fast. Don't worry, Charleigh. My brothers and I will take care of this. We are meeting with the *Pakhan* and his people in an hour."

"What does he have to do with this?"

"I'm not sure yet. It's possible he's aware that your sister is being used as a pawn by Dimitri. We'll know more soon."

The *Pakhan* knows about my sister? How did she ever get on his radar?

Dimitri.

If he or any of his people lay a finger on Evie, I will make sure they suffer, so help me God. One way or the other.

But first things first. I know I have to let Niko and his brothers take care of things their own way. They'd better not take long, though. I won't wait.

Not when my sister's well-being is at stake.

As the adrenaline rush slows, a sadness trickles through me, a heartbreaking sadness, where I remember how vulnerable Evie was right after Mother died. The poor kid couldn't do anything. She was catatonic, completely regressed. I had to help her bathe, get dressed, even comb her own hair. Granted, she was only six, but she had developed some self-care skills that were all gone overnight.

It was heartbreaking. It *is* heartbreaking. A six-year-old should not have to suffer like that.

But then, neither should a ten-year-old. I was hardly mature enough to take care of myself, never mind a little sister.

My shoulders shake as the tears come.

Why?

Why did my life turn into this?

Is it all my father's carelessness?

Or did I do something to deserve it?

Actually, no. No one deserves the level of shit life has thrown my way. It's not fair.

Not. Fucking. Fair.

Niko looks at his watch. "You wait here, Charleigh, okay? I'll be right back after the meeting and we'll devise a plan."

Wiping at tears with my shirt sleeve, I nod. I know I look like a mess. I don't give a damn.

"Thank you, Niko. Thank you for helping with Evie."

I don't bother mentioning that if he and his brothers hadn't barged their way into my life, none of this ever would have happened.

What would be the point of bringing that up?

When he leaves, I take a deep breath and get to my feet. I pace the room, hoping some movement will straighten out my thoughts.

I know of one arcade in town. It's not in the best neighborhood, and if I remember correctly, it's a hangout for exactly the sort of people Niko described.

He wants me to wait so he and his brothers can make a move. They don't want to show their hand, at least not too soon. I get that.

But it's my *sister*.

I could run over there. Just take a quick look. Get the lay of the land. She's probably not even there right now, it's the middle of the school day.

But I can't get out without Frank by my side, and he sure as hell isn't going to let me walk into any trouble.

Unless he doesn't know yet. Unless he doesn't know about my sister hanging out at the arcade.

And if he doesn't know, he can't object to my going over there.

Just to check the place out.

That's all.

I swear.

CHAPTER THIRTY-NINE

*K*IR

"It is time you—"

I ignore the *Pakhan's* second in command, the imperious little shit. He has some balls, trying to tell my brothers and me what we will or won't do. He's nothing but a lackey, a trouble making son of a bitch.

Fuck him.

Simultaneously, the three of us turn our backs on him and focus on the *Pakhan*. He's the only one who matters.

Although his 'second' would probably contest that.

Hierarchies exist for a reason in our world, and while the second might be trying to test the boundaries of that, we Alekseevs are not buying it. He has no authority over us, no matter how much he wishes he did.

Funny thing is, we grew up around all these people we now work with. We played together as kids, our parents vacationed together, and our fathers ran businesses together. And here we are, a generation later, carrying on the trade, so to speak.

But relationships change. When there are competing objectives at play, it's bound to happen. Unfortunately, a lot of that starts with Dimitri. If he were only able to accept being passed over by his father, which I am sure sucked for him, he wouldn't harbor this endless resentment against my brothers and me. He wouldn't be making trouble, acting as if he's 'owed' anything, much less our girl Charleigh.

Which is basically why we are here today.

The *Pakhan* sits back in the chair behind his huge desk, not having offered a seat to my brothers and me. That's okay, though. It's a power thing, and he's allowed to exercise that. Besides, he's not happy with us today.

Can't blame him.

We are openly defying him. This is seen as disrespect. And disrespect doesn't go over well in our world.

"I told you your girl—whatever her name is—belongs to Dimitri now," he says matter-of-factly.

Right. He doesn't even know Charleigh's name. Couldn't give a shit. In his world—the old world— women are nothing but chattel.

Not that I, or any of us, should talk. I mean, the whole concept of the club, as created by Papa, is about permitting men to let off steam with beautiful women. But I like to think these women have some agency.

Maybe not as much as they would like, but I am damn sure my generation treats them better than Papa's did. Which is why what happened to Stacey has been so heavy on my mind the last day, even though Charleigh thinks we don't care.

I have no doubt that if my brothers and I had been around, Dominika would not have been as generous with Stacey, offering her to Alexei on a silver platter since he was pissed that he lost out on Charleigh.

When she went missing, the men waiting to bid on her assumed she'd be back up for auction as soon as she returned. That didn't happen. My brothers and I decided that wasn't the right path for Charleigh, and most of our members under- stood. They trust us to run our business as we see fit.

But Alexei wants what he wants. He's not used to being told no. After we questioned Dominika, it's clear she knew he'd take his frustrations out on the poor girl.

If that's not fucked up, I don't know what is. We need to remedy this but must proceed carefully. Alexei still has a lot of power in our world.

And then there's Dominika, but first, we need to take care of this Charleigh situation, once and for all.

We haven't seen much of Dimitri lately. That could be a good or bad thing. Either he's laying low because he's got some other distraction going on, which is good news for us—we're always happy to have him out of our hair—or he's got something up his sleeve, something designed to let us know how unhappy he is with us.

His grievances are certainly behind today's meeting with the *Pakhan*. I'm surprised Dimitri's not here to gloat in our faces, although the second seems to be taking care of that for him.

Too bad we are ignoring the fucker.

"Charleigh Gates is her name, sir, and with all respect due to you, we have other plans for her. She is not available to Dimitri, nor anybody else."

The *Pakhan* hides his surprise at our defiance, but I know it's there. Men like him are not used to being contradicted. He's thrown off.

Not that he'd ever let on. At least outwardly.

But *I* know. I may not be able to see it, but it's in the air. I can smell it. I can feel it. And the man is not happy.

The second muscles his way back into our field of vision, as if he's been part of the conversation all along.

I could be cordial with him, but I just can't make myself throw a drop of respect his way. It's not going to happen.

He puffs his chest up. "The *Pakhan* has decreed you will hand this woman over to Dimitri. There is nothing to be discussed. It has been decided," he declares.

We don't look at him, never mind acknowledge his demands, which further infuriates him. The *Pakhan*, however, doesn't seem to notice. Or if he does, he doesn't care.

"Sir, we are prepared to make monetary restitution for keeping the woman to ourselves," Vadik says in a calm, even tone that indicates our decision is not open for discussion.

Fortunately for us, this intrigues the *Pakhan*. He's a man like all of us here, and is not immune to being bought, at least not when the price is right.

The second takes up position next to the *Pakhan* like they're on the same team or something. Which I suppose they are. But he doesn't have to stand shoulder-to-shoulder with his boss to prove it.

"You have insulted the *Pakhan* with your insubordination. That is not acceptable," he barks.

But the *Pakhan* waves him away. "I want to hear what the Alekseevs have in mind. If a payment is made to me, and an apology sent to Dimitri, I think we can consider this case closed."

Inwardly, I breathe a sigh of relief. I'd never let on, but I was not entirely sure which way this would go, and whether the *Pakhan* could be swayed with an offer of monetary compensation.

Turns out he can, like most everyone.

But this doesn't work for his second. "Sir, that is not the proper approach. These men need to abide by your ruling," he barks.

The *Pakhan,* who has looked only at my brothers and me since this meeting started, slowly rotates his head to see his second. "You do not have a vote here, particularly since you are a friend of Dimitri's. You are biased, like I already told you."

After his scolding, the *Pakhan* turns back to us and doesn't see, like I do, the red rage all over the second's face.

Humiliation never feels good, but at the hands of your boss hurts like fucking hell, and in front of others is excruciating. And now he can't do Dimitri's bidding, having essentially been de-balled by his boss. Any credibility he had has flown out the door. I always knew the bastard was biased. I just didn't know how much.

Many of us in this world are friends in one way or another. An important part of our job is to not let that color our decisions. Some of us are better at it than others. Obviously.

"We will work out details of compensation at a later meeting," the *Pakhan* says, looking at his watch, "but send Dimitri an apology. And then, I don't want to hear anything else about this. We all have more important matters to attend to."

He throws a side-eye at his second, who nods his acceptance almost imperceptibly. The man's ready to explode. It's written all over his ugly face.

But he doesn't say a thing. He can't if he wants to stay alive.

One of the first things Papa taught me about this business is knowing when to shut your damn mouth. Guess the second missed that day at criminal school.

Dimitri won't be happy, either, which thrills the petty side of me to no end. Another battle won by the Alekseevs, bringing us closer to winning the war.

The war we have with Dimitri, kicked off by age-old grievances, escalated by his murder of our parents.

We may have to make an apology to the man, but he's not long for this world anyway. If we wait long enough, we may never have to deliver.

CHAPTER FORTY

The limo is quiet on the ride back to the club. I suppose we're lost in thought, glad to get back to real business and stop thinking about Dimitri, wasting everyone's time with his trivial gripes. Although I don't put it past him to try some new sort of shit with us. The man is like a poorly-trained pit bull. He just doesn't know when to let go.

The day will come when we show him. Of course, that's the day he'll take his last breath.

I touch the claw marks left on my neck by Charleigh a few days prior. I know my brothers noticed them, but no one said anything.

There was nothing to say. They know where they're from. They know why they're there.

Charleigh, our sweet and beautiful Charleigh, was working through some bad times.

Actually, she's not done. Not sure she ever will be. We all get our share of life's shit sandwich. I know I have. And Charleigh's had a big dose of that unpleasantness, maybe more than one person deserves.

She's earned the right to go off her rocker every now and then.

"I feel like we haven't treated Charleigh right," I say, doing my best to temper the hesitation in my voice.

I have no idea how my brothers will react to this and I want to broach the subject carefully. I wait for their wrath, or should I say, Vadik's wrath.

Niko, the sensitive, mellow one, is not inclined to blow up over anything. So I guess, when it comes down to it, I'm more concerned about Vadik's reaction. But this is a conversation we need to have.

Charleigh is important to me.

She's important to all of us. I just want to find out to what extent.

"You're right, Kir," Niko says without hesitation.

Maybe he was thinking of bringing up the subject, too?

"I don't know that I see Dominika's actions as maliciously-intended as Charleigh does, but I don't like that she feels as if she hasn't been listened to by us."

Niko. Always the diplomat.

"I want to make it up to her," he adds.

Niko and I bounce ideas back and forth about ways to show Charleigh she is respected and valued, and it feels good. It feels good because it's going to make our girl feel good.

But Vadik doesn't agree and he makes that clear. "Guys, would you both shut the hell up. You sound like fucking middle-school boys with a crush on the prettiest girl in class."

Leave it to Vadik to put a damper on a party.

"We owe her nothing. As it is, we saved her from the auction. She's still our property. We just haven't decided yet what we are doing with her," he says in a heated voice.

Niko and I glance at each other. We don't usually contradict Vadik when he's at his worst, but this might just be the perfect time.

He's not finished with his vitriol yet. "She interfered with our business, she defied us, she made us look bad. Don't make her out to be some sort of saint. She's an asset of ours. Nothing more," he says with finality.

In his finality, I hear a hesitation. It was split-second, for sure, and anyone who doesn't know my brother like I do might have missed it.

I didn't, though, and a glance at Niko indicates he heard the same.

Vadik might blow a lot of hot air and act like he doesn't care about Charleigh, but I am not buying it. In fact, I am pretty sure he's full of shit, not least of which because he gave her that expensive bracelet. I'm not going to call him out though, at least not directly, but I see the doubt in his words. I hear them. And he does too.

Niko takes a long inhale through his nose. I know he's about to drop a bombshell. And boy, does he.

"Say what you like, Vadik. She's nobody's property."

Niko's right. And we all need to admit how we feel about her. It's on the tip of my tongue when Niko beats me to it.

"I love her. I am in love with her. And I think you guys are too."

CHAPTER FORTY-ONE

I'm silent on the drive over to Evie's school. I had to twist Frank's arm to agree to come with me, and I don't want to risk saying anything to make him change his mind and demand I turn Niko's car around and head back to the club.

Without seeing my sister.

I glance at the clock on the car's dashboard and see there are just a few minutes before Charleigh's school breaks for lunch. I want to get there before she leaves the campus to get something to eat. If I miss her coming out the door, it will be much harder to find her in the throng of noisy teenagers. I pull up just as the bell rings and the upperclassmen exercise their ability to leave campus to do whatever they want for sixty minutes. I'm aware these kids can exit not only the school's front door but also any of the side and back doors, but I also know Evie favors the front, so it's my best bet to wait here.

Leaving Frank in the car, I huddle on the sidewalk with the few parents picking up their kids at the day's halfway mark for a variety of reasons like visits to the orthodontist and the like. It's when the last stragglers exit, and all the parents are gone, having collected their charges, that I realize I won't be seeing Evie, at least not here.

I turn to give Frank the 'one minute' signal with my finger and jog up the school steps. Through the intercom I explain I'm looking for my sister, and since I've been to the school on so many occasions, they let me right in.

"Hi, Mrs. Bellamy," I say to the ancient front office secretary, the same woman holding down the fort as when I was there.

She smiles kindly, like always. "Miss Gates, hello. Looking for our little Evie, are you?"

I think fast. "Yes. I got her a last-minute dentist appointment. I'm sorry we didn't give you more notice."

Mrs. Bellamy creases her brow and flips through a huge three-ring notebook that looks like it holds all the school's secrets. While it seems like she's not finding what she wants, she smiles again, and excuses herself, heading for the principal's office.

A pit drops in my stomach. Something's not right. Mrs. Bellamy would normally tell me that Evie must be at lunch with her friends. But when she opened her giant notebook, I knew something was up.

"Miss Gates," she says, placing her hands on the counter between us when she returns from the principal's office, "Evie didn't come to school today. We were about to call you to see if she was with you."

CHAPTER FORTY-TWO

CHARLEIGH

My heart slams against my chest as I run out the school door and back to the car. I take my place behind the steering wheel and grip it until my knuckles are white.

"What's going on?" Frank asks.

God, I just want to smack that kid. "She skipped today. Skipped school."

Frank runs his giant fingers over his chin. "Jesus. Okay, let's get back to the club. It's not going to do us any good to wait here."

I turn in my seat to face him. He needs to know how serious I am. "Frank, we need to go to the arcade. I bet that's where she is. Please, Frank, let's pop by there and see if we can find her."

But he shakes his head, *no*. "No can do, Charleigh. The guys would have my balls. It's bad news over there and you can't go until they've cleared a few things up. It's not safe."

I pause a moment so I don't freak out. It doesn't help, and I slam my hand on the console between us.

"Frank!" I say shrilly, "my *sister* could be there. I know it's not safe for me and maybe not even you, and if that's the case, it sure as hell isn't safe for *her* to be there."

He looks out the car window at Evie's high school, which used to be my high school, and sighs deeply. "If I get fired, this is on you."

I put the car in *drive*. "You won't get fired, Frank, promise," I say, steering the car toward a part of town I'd normally never visit.

In an otherwise deserted strip mall, the arcade turns out to be a junky little storefront that makes Pops's pawn shop look high end. The front glass has been spray-painted for privacy by someone attempting to achieve an artsy graffiti-type look, but who was really only capable of creating something that looks finger-painted by a kindergartner.

Heads turn as I park near the entrance and then weave through the people, all tough-looking boys and girls, hanging out on the front steps smoking cigarettes. These are the kind of kids I was afraid of when I was younger. Hell, they're still scary. But I have Frank with me, and he could squash any of them with his thumb. I look back over my shoulder to where he's waiting in the car. He nods at me. He has my back.

He's a good guy. The Alekseevs are lucky to have him. *I'm* lucky to have him.

When I get to the door, I'm stopped by a bouncer.

What kind of arcade has a bouncer?

"Can I help you, miss?" a huge man with a tattooed face says, yawning with boredom while he looks me up and down.

"Hey, I just want to run in and see if my sister's inside. I'll be right back out," I say while I continue to move toward the door like it's a forgone conclusion I'm going in.

He nods and pushes it open, pulling it closed once I'm inside.

It's dark except for the blinking lights of the games and it takes a moment for my eyes to adjust. I am immediately assaulted with the sounds of an arcade—the pinging of points being earned, the sound of virtual cars crashing, and the grunts of teenage boys losing to their friends.

It only takes me a minute to find the boy who was in the photo with Evie.

I tap him on the arm and he looks at me,

surprised to see someone my age in the arcade. And I'm only freaking twenty.

"What?" he asks with a sneer.

Glad to know my sister's hanging out with high-quality people.

"I know you from somewhere," I say with a smile and flip of my hair. "Don't you remember me?" I ask, shimmying my shoulders.

This grabs his attention and his demeanor instantly changes. "Oh, um, yeah. I remember you," he says cockily, looking me up and down.

"I knew it," I laugh, brushing his bicep with my fingertips. "I'm Charleigh. What's your name again?"

He puffs his chest out a little. Were boys so predictable when I was a teenager?

"I'm Arseny." I could swear he deepened his voice when he said that.

As if on cue.

I slap my thigh. "Right! Arseny. Such a cool name, I don't know how I forgot it. I think you said it was… wait… Russian, right?" I ask, shaking a finger in his face.

He beams. "Yup. Sure is. My parents are off the boat," he says.

Yeah, they're probably criminals too, like everyone else I spend my time with.

But I nod enthusiastically. "Hey, I met a girl here the other day named Evie. You know her?"

A shadow crosses his face, like he's been busted. He wanted to play us both?

Idiot.

"Yeah. She's over there," he says, pointing with his thumb.

"I'm gonna go say hi. You sticking around here for a while?"

"For sure," he says, grinning.

Good. Very good.

I weave through the labyrinth of noisy electronic games. They are played mostly by boys, with the occasional girl scattered among them, hanging around like a juvenile version of arm candy. They're learning early, these girls.

That's when I spot my sister—at the exact same moment she spots me.

Her mouth drops open and she jerks as if to run away.

Really?

I reach for her. "Evie."

"Um, what are you doing here?" she demands, raising her voice when she sees her friends wondering why she's talking to me.

Show time for Evie.

"I've come to get you," I say quietly. No need to embarrass the kid.

"No!" she screams, looking at her friends to make sure they're watching her performance.

She backs up like I'm some kind of monster.

"Is something wrong, Evie?" Arseny asks from behind me.

"Oh my God, Arseny, help me," she cries, brushing past and jumping into his arms.

The other kids gather around us, eager for a fight or some kind of drama. I'm not surprised, given they're nearly all drinking Red Bull and are surrounded by a racket that would push most people over the edge.

Arseny grabs Evie tightly, then points a finger at me. "You think I don't know who you are, don't you?" he laughs.

Evie looks up at him, surprised. "You know my sister? How do you know my sister, Arseny?"

She looks between the two of us, confused.

"I knew who she was before she even walked in here, before she started flirting with me like a whore," he spits.

Nice guy, just like his uncle, Dimitri.

And as if on cue, who appears from behind a row of Mortal Combat machines?

Fucking Dimitri.

And his crew, who strategically position themselves between me and the door.

Goddammit. I wonder if I've been gone long enough for Frank to come look for me? Actually, I'm sure I have been. Where the hell is he?

Arseny shoves my sister toward me.

"Hey," she cries, "what are you doing?"

She shoots back to him, but he puts up his hands like a warning. "Don't come running to me, fool. I'm not your savior."

A ripple of laughter flits through the crowd as confusion crosses Evie's face.

"What… what do you mean, Arseny?" she asks, her bottom lip twitching.

Evie might be slow on the uptake, but it's clear to me that I've been set up. Actually, she has too. She was used to get to me, although I doubt she's in any danger.

Me, I'm a different story.

I inch toward the exit but Dimitri's men conveniently spread out to block any chance I might have at escape.

With no other option, I take the direct route. I get up in Dimitri's face. I'm scared, of course, but I'm also pissed. Pissed that these creeps messed with my younger sister to get to me, and pissed that I have to look over my shoulder everywhere I go.

First, it was the Alekseev brothers, and now it's him.

Who will it be next week? Alexei?

Or someone different altogether?

A month ago none of these people would have given me a second look. Now they all want me?

Which is the most absurd, infuriating thing I can imagine.

I don't know whether I should roll around on the floor laughing or double over in tears. That's how fucked all this is.

Me.

I'm nothing. I'm nobody. I have nothing to offer people in this world.

I'm just a girl trying to make her way in life. I don't need this shit.

"What the hell do you want with me?" I scream in Dimitri's face, close enough I can smell the greasy shit he puts in his hair.

His flunkies surround us as if I'm going to take him out.

A slow smile spreads across Dimitri's face, and he studies me. "You're even more beautiful close up," he breathes.

This again?

"Dimitri, can we be real with each other?" I ask, and a titter of laughter runs through the audience that's assembled.

None of whom, by the way, offer any sort of help to either my whimpering sister or me.

And Frank is still nowhere to be seen.

"Yes, baby?" he says.

My stomach roils with nausea, but I won't let myself take a step back. I have to be strong and stand up to this lame excuse for a human being.

"Can't you leave me alone? I've done nothing to you. I have nothing to offer you. What is all this setup bullshit about?" I ask, gesturing at my sister and the crowd behind me.

"Oh, but that's where you're wrong, *zolotse*. You have so much to offer me. And those terrible Alekseev boys have kept you from me. But no more. You're mine now, and you're going to see just how much you can give to a man like me. And if you don't want to give, give me everything I want," he says with a dramatic shrug, "then I will just take. And take, and take, and take."

Without thinking, I wind up my arm to smack his ugly face. But his team get to me before I can hit him.

He lets his head drop back, his mouth wide open, and a booming laughter fills the air. When he's done, he narrows his eyes, his mirth of moments before completely gone. He scowls, and in an instant grabs a huge hank of hair on the back of my head, jerking it until my neck is bent at an unnatural and painful angle.

"D…Dimitri…" I sputter.

He cuts me off. "You act like you're so special, under the protection of those Alekseev fuckers. But you're just the daughter of a loser pawn shop owner. You're just—what do they call it here in America? —*white trash*," he hisses, saliva spraying my face.

There is a scream and sudden movement in the crowd and it takes me a moment, but I see Evie trying to get to me by pounding on one of Dimitri's guards. I can't see much because of how my head is tilted but when he stops her with one huge, blocky arm, she dives for his hand and bites it until he screams.

Another guard picks her up from behind and finally gets her to release the hand she's biting

Her fury shocks me.

"Let my sister go!" she screams, thrashing in the arms of another thug.

"Shut up, you little bitch," Dimitri roars, and she quiets, tears pouring down her distorted face.

"Let her go, Dimitri. She's just a kid. Please. I'll do anything. Just don't hurt her," I plead.

"Don't worry, I have no interest in that little punk. It's you I want. We're going to have lots of fun together, *zolotse*. And you will do anything I want you to. I plan to fuck every hole in your body before I'm done with you and then maybe see if my boys here would like a little taste of American white trash."

Vile. The man is vile. And when he releases his hold on my head, I stand there in front of him. Defeated. Empty. Done.

As they lead me out of the arcade I take a last look at Evie, screaming and sobbing and reaching for me. Just like she did when she was six years old and was having nightmares about our mother.

We pass Niko's car and when I'm close enough I can see Frank, still in the passenger seat. And I know why he didn't come to help.

He's slumped over the central console, a trickle of blood on the side of his head.

Oh, Frank.

I am responsible for all this. I should have just stayed at the club and let the brothers take care of finding my sister and keeping Dimitri at bay.

But no. I couldn't wait. The minute the Alekseevs left, I pestered Frank to let me look for Evie.

Dimitri opens the car door, and I politely climb in with no thought for resisting, or plan to escape.

What would be the point? So I can keep running? And he can keep chasing?

I put my seatbelt on like a nice girl and look straight ahead.

Any fight I ever had?

It's gone now.

CHAPTER FORTY-THREE

Glad we got that shit off our backs.

Now that the *Pakhan* is happy with our compensation and apology, the matter of Dimitri taking Charleigh is settled.

Over. Finalized. Complete.

I can get back to worrying about important things like keeping the club running, as well as our other businesses.

And trying to figure out what to do about the lovely Charleigh.

Who, apparently, Niko is in love with. And Kir too, although he hasn't said as much.

That leaves me, and not in a good place. Because, fuck all, for as much as I bluster about her being our property and shit, I'm falling for her too. Not good.

Not at all. Not for our business, and not for me. She's not the right woman for me. Neither is she for my brothers. But I can't tell them what to do about love.

Maybe I'll take a trip. Get out of town for a little while. Even go to that Russian matchmaker my mother was always shoving down my throat. Get married to the spoiled daughter of another leader in the vast world of Russian criminals, produce a few offspring, and sow my oats with mistresses just like Papa did.

Back from our meeting with the *Pakhan*, my brothers and I exit the elevator on the top floor of the club, and we each head to our respective offices. Before I reach mine, I run into Dominika.

"How was your meeting with the *Pakhan*?" she asks.

How the hell did she know we had a meeting with the *Pakhan*? And why does she need to know about it?

I consider putting her in her place, but I'm happy with how things went, my consternation about my brothers and Charleigh aside, so I turn to her with a smile. "Very well, thank you for asking."

She nods politely. "Say, Vadik, do you know where Charleigh is? I wanted to ask her how Stacey is. I figure she knows."

Yeah, like Dominika gives a shit about Stacey.

I shake my head. "She's probably around some-where. Did you call her cell?"

Dominika nods. "Yes, I did. Frank's too."

My stomach turns and a burning sensation shoots up the back of my throat. The last time I felt like this was when I found out my parents were dead.

"Are… you sure?" I ask, pulling out my own phone and dialing both numbers.

Neither of which are answered.

What the fuck?

Leaving Dominika, I run down the hall, reaching Kir's office first. "Charleigh is missing. And so is Frank."

He drops what he's doing and jumps to his feet.

I turn for Niko's office, but he's already right in front of me.

"I heard you. What's going on?"

I shake my head. "We need to find out, as quickly as possible."

If she fucking left again, I will lose my mind. I don't need this bullshit. This girl is not worth it, I don't care how in love with her my brothers are.

Or how unique, lovely, sweet, innocent, intelli-gent, and sexy she is.

No. None of those things matter.

"I got something," Niko says, tapping his phone. "I tracked my car's GPS. It's parked across town. How did it get there?"

He clicks again, and his app zeroes in on an address offering a view of some sort of business. He taps a few more times and zooms in on a store front sign.

"Arcade? Are they at an arcade?" I ask, frowning.

Niko groans. "Fuck. Her sister has been hanging out in an arcade. Charleigh wanted to go get her, but I told her to let us take care of it."

"So she went even though you told her not to," Kir says.

Niko closes his eyes, and his lips press into a long, thin line. He is not happy.

None of us are.

What the fuck, Charleigh?

How the hell can we keep this woman safe if she keeps making bad decisions and walking into dangerous situations?

Without a word, the three of us head for the elevator, Kir repeatedly pressing the *down* button like that will make it come faster.

CHAPTER FORTY-FOUR

Vadik

The tension in the car is noxious as we drive across town in silence.

It's clear we're all thinking through possible scenarios to explain where the hell Charleigh and Frank might be, and why the fuck Niko's car is in an arcade parking lot. It's my guess we're keeping our thoughts to ourselves to avoid arguing. I know I'm not ready to share my theory. It's one that won't go over well with my brothers, who are probably banking on something totally different.

Niko, who is more attached to Charleigh than anyone—well, maybe he's not more attached, but he's more vocal about it—most likely thinks the worst, that something bad has happened to her.

As I drive, I can see him in the rear-view mirror.

He hasn't stopped drumming his fingers or chewing on his bottom lip since we left the club. For his sake, I hope Charleigh is okay. I'm not sure how he'll handle it, otherwise. He tries to hide it but he's a sensitive soul, at least more sensitive than Kir, and certainly a bastard like me. While he's twenty-six and has dated plenty of beautiful women, he has yet to meet his 'true love' as he cheesily puts it.

I hope for his sake this true love is not Charleigh, but it might be a little too late to prevent that.

Kir, on the other hand, is probably just thinking Charleigh's out having fun somewhere and either lost her phone or let it run out of battery. How that explains Frank's absence doesn't fit at all, but Kir's never been a detail guy.

A sidelong glance at him in the passenger seat shows him bopping his head to the music playing on the radio. He's humming and when he knows a few words, sings along off-key. I bet that in his mind, Charleigh will reappear at any moment and all will be well. For Kir more than anyone, I want Charleigh to be okay. His losing Clara in the car accident has weighed so heavily on him over the years I doubt he could handle losing another woman he cares for. He hasn't talked about her death in a while but the first couple years after she died were brutal. We barely left him alone for fear of what he might do to himself.

As for myself, I'm a lying son of a bitch if I don't admit I have a thing for Charleigh, just like my brothers do. However, I am more cynical than they are, and to put it simply, I'd wager that Charleigh has taken off again. She doesn't want to be part of our criminal organization and the ups and downs that come with it. It probably doesn't help that after she returned from her latest attempt to take off, we were pretty harsh with her.

I thought all those bad feelings had blown over.

Before we snatched her from her father's pawn shop, she was on her own path. She wanted to be a Chicago office girl, living quietly and simply. Sure, the luxe accommodations, clothing, and gifts we give her are a nice novelty, but things like that do little for a woman like her. She wants to make her own way in an honest manner. I'm not sure that's going to happen after the time she's spent with us, but I love her for wanting it.

Fuck. *Love*.

I might be as screwed as my brothers. But I am about a thousand percent more realistic. Charleigh is smart and resourceful. If she wants to get away from us and never be found, she'll find a way to make that happen. I think our most recent encounter with her might just have been our last.

My brothers aren't thinking this yet. Too painful. So I'm not bringing it up. Why intentionally crush someone's hopes? I may be a fucker of the highest degree, but I also care about these guys. I'm not about to shit all over them with my suspicions.

We pull into the parking lot where Niko's car should be and sure enough, spot it immediately. But because we're not sure what's going on and must be on the lookout for traps, we idle my car in the far side of the lot, as far away as we can be but still see it.

"I'm not waiting," Niko says, grabbing the door handle.

"Hold on!" I bark. Stay calm, I tell myself. Pulling the big brother thing on Niko could very well blow up in my face. "It's not going to do anyone any good if there's someone watching the car, waiting for us to come along."

He chews his bottom lip, and I can see he's close to losing his shit. I have to get him under control.

I lost both my parents two years ago. I won't lose a brother, not before his time, anyway.

"Nik, look at me. Stay with me, man. I know you're torn up on the inside. But we need to be smart about this."

His hand tightens on the door handle, but he doesn't pull. Not that he won't, he just won't at this very moment.

As we watch, a couple kids wander in and out of the arcade, grabbing a smoke on the front steps. Others come and go, arriving and leaving on foot or via one of the many BMX bikes locked to the stair railing in the absence of a real bike rack. It's a dingy, trashy place, and I can't believe Charleigh would come here unless she was sure her sister was here.

I dial her phone again and then Frank's, because I'm tired of tapping my fingers on the steering wheel. I'm worked up. I can't deny it, goddammit.

The kids, mostly boys, are boisterous and seem to know each other. They slap each other on the back in greeting like they're badasses or something, and I suppose in their little worlds maybe they are.

The good news is they've taken no notice of us, they're so caught up in themselves.

"I'll tell you guys what," I say, putting the car in *drive*, "I'm going to slowly cruise by Niko's car. We'll be more protected this way if there's anything to worry about, and we can make a fast escape if necessary."

"Do it," Kir says, nodding.

Niko remains silent. I know the poor bastard is in agony.

We cross the parking lot, not too quickly nor too slowly, not wanting to attract unnecessary attention from either the punks hanging out, or anyone who might be watching for us.

And in getting closer to Niko's car, we see all we need to know.

I'm a cold-hearted fucker and to my surprise, my heart thumps hard, my pulse racing. While I still maintain that Charleigh has just taken off, I am also in fear for her.

Frank is in the car. But he's not alive.

He's slumped over the seat in such a way that he's impossible to see until close up, closer than we were on the other side of the parking lot. The telltale trickle of blood on his temple proves someone who knows their way around a gun took care of him.

Goddammit.

And where is Charleigh?

Frank may have been killed for any number of reasons, but if Charleigh took off like I think she did, is she responsible for killing him?

I don't see it. I just don't see her killing him, or anyone. That would mean someone else did it, most likely to get to Charleigh.

Niko and Kir are silent as I make another circle around the car, and the kids hanging out are starting to take notice of us.

Niko speaks in a slow, deliberate tone. "I don't think she's in there. I think she *was*, but she no longer is. Her sister was hanging out with a kid who I'm pretty sure was Dimitri's nephew."

Holy fuck. That's all I need to know. I want to get out of here before the kids wander over and see Frank dead for themselves, so I hightail it out of the lot and jump on the freeway.

"Jesus fucking Christ," Kir says quietly.

"Go to her dad's place," Niko barks. "I want to talk to Gil Gates. See what he knows."

"On the way," I say.

But Gil Gates is useless, as he always is. Not only does he not know where Charleigh is, he doesn't even know where Evie, his youngest, is.

We get back in the car, disgusted with how checked out he is.

"What the fuck is wrong with that guy?" Kir asks no one in particular.

He's right to ask. Something is up with that man. I want to get to the bottom of it, but that will have to wait for another day.

Right now, our priority is Charleigh.

"What about Victoria's house? The woman she stayed with the first time she ran?" Kir suggests.

I turn the car in that direction, but don't hold

much hope that Victoria knows anything. And if she did, I doubt she'd tell us anyway.

When she doesn't answer her door, we head back to the club. Driving around aimlessly is not going to do us any good. Niko makes a call to someone who will get the car at the arcade, and make sure it's cleaned top to bottom. What they will do with Frank, I don't know. I can't worry about that right now.

At a traffic light I rub the bridge of my nose between my forefinger and thumb, waiting for my usual stress migraine to make itself known, and when I feel a twitch at the back of my skull, a muscle contracting, I know I'm in for a doozy.

"Maybe it's just as well that she's gone," Niko mumbles so quietly I barely hear him.

Fuck me. Words I never thought would come out of that man's mouth. He has a point though, and I join him in wondering the same.

From the corner of my eye, I see Kir nod. "Things have been pretty fucked since she came on the scene. Niko's right. We don't need her kind of distraction."

Holy shit. My brothers are throwing in the towel.

Are they just being pussies, giving up before they get really hurt by this woman? Is this a defensive move on their part?

Or do they really believe she's gone for good?

"Guys, personally, I still think she might have run." But I don't sound convinced. Because I am not. I want to believe that, rather than think she's in Dimitri's or anyone else's clutches.

But for Frank to be dead, she's probably with someone who wanted her very, very badly.

There's only one person who fits that description.

My brothers join the conversation, but I'm not really listening as they go back and forth about where Charleigh might be and what they want to do about it. All I can think is that the thought of not seeing her again does not feel good, not at all, and that maybe I need to be honest with myself for once, just once, and acknowledge that this woman has gotten under my skin.

And into my heart.

CHAPTER FORTY-FIVE

CHARLEIGH

"Happy birthday, honey."

Mother's soothing voice fills my ears and I turn over to sleep for a few minutes more, a contented smile on my face.

I've always wondered whether my mother was *really* dead, and now it appears she's not, thank goodness. But I don't ask where she's been. I don't want to hurt her feelings, that all this time we thought she was gone, she's been right here with us all along. We just couldn't see her. Or something like that.

I also don't tell her that today is *not* my birthday. Again, I don't want to hurt her feelings, and besides, she's been out of sight for so long it feels good to hear her voice even if she does have the date wrong.

It's been one of the hardest things, at least it was when I was little, to have a birthday pass with no wishes from her. My dad would sing Happy Birthday on the years he remembered, which were few. But it was nothing like Mother, who would wake me up with a treat of hot chocolate, which she let me drink in bed, and a breakfast of blueberry pancakes with so much maple syrup she would laugh and say she was surprised I didn't drink it straight out of the bottle.

"Hey," a coarse voice, a male voice says. There's a rough hand on my shoulder and someone shakes me twice.

It must be a mistake. I'm here with my mother. And I want to stay with her. So I don't open my eyes. I'm not ready to wake up.

Back in my dream, Mother takes her time and brushes out my hair in long, graceful strokes while I watch out the kitchen window into the backyard where the family dog barks at a squirrel in a tree.

Everything is so perfect, so ultimately, exquisitely perfect that, while Mother starts on my French braids, I close my eyes to better hear her, smell her, and feel her gentle fingers.

But a sharp tug on my hair tells me all is not what I thought. Mother would never pull my hair. I don't know why she is now.

I force my eyes to open and the first thing I realize, besides my room not being bathed in the sunlight it was a moment ago in the bliss of my dream, is that I can't move. I mean, I can move, but to do so is excruciatingly painful.

What is going on?

My eyes focus at least partially and I realize Mother does not have her fingers in my hair but rather some man does, a man who is looking at me with disgust. Contempt. Disrespect. Even loathing.

What's happening? I want to ask. But then I realize moving my lips feels strange, and the odd taste in my mouth is not Mother's hot chocolate but something metallic and salty.

And disgusting.

I close my eyes again and see Mother. I reach out but can't get to her. She's walking away from me, getting smaller and smaller, and eventually I can't even see her bright yellow sweater any longer.

Why did she leave? Did I do something wrong?

"Goddammit, wake up," the coarse voice demands.

I open my eyes but can't see very well. It's like I'm wearing a mask where one eye is completely covered and the other is just a skinny little slit. I raise my arm to take the mask off, unsure why the person waking me up is so impatient, and as I reach, my back screams in pain and I scream in response, falling back on the bed the way I was when Mother was waking me up.

I close my eyes again and search for Mother, but there is no sign of her yellow sweater, no sign that she's coming back to finish braiding my hair or wishing me happy birthday.

She *has* to finish my hair. I can't go to school with it half-braided.

"Come on!" the man yells again, and this time scoops an arm under my shoulders and forces me to a sitting position. Something about the movement is terribly painful, and I wonder why I can't just keep sleeping.

I look at one of my hands through the mask I'm wearing. My fingernails are broken and coated in what looks like blood. I look down at myself and I'm pretty sure I'm in the same clothes I had on two days ago, which is weird, because Mother picks out fresh clothes for us each day.

"M… Mother?" I mumble.

This makes the man laugh. "Your mother ain't here, honey. And she ain't coming, either."

I gradually lift one hand to my face in order to remove the mask and realize there is none, and that my face is puffed up in strangely unfamiliar bumps that hurt like hell. My eye, the one I can't see out of, is so puffy it won't open, and the other is nearly as bad.

That's why I can't see—I don't have a mask on—there's something wrong with my face.

As the man pulls me to my feet, I realize there's also something wrong with my legs, which buckle under me before he lets go.

"Come on. You can stand," he says.

"Why are you doing this? It's my birthday," I murmur.

Shouldn't he be nice to me on my birthday? Mother always says birthdays are special and that everyone should be extra nice to you on your special day.

The man just laughs. "It's not your birthday, honey. Far from it. Come on now. We're going downstairs."

I take a few stumbling steps, leaning heavily on the man, who seems irritated at having to support me.

He shouldn't be mean to me. It's my birthday. He just doesn't know.

"Where are we going?" I murmur as the man and I approach a blurry car.

"You're going home," he says.

"No," I moan. "I *am* home. And I want to go back

to bed. It's my birthday. And my mother is doing my hair…" I taper off.

But the man lays me down in the backseat of a car anyway and doesn't tell me where we're going. All I know is that I want to go back to Mother, whether it was a dream or not, and that I have no shoes on and my feet are cold.

I go back to sleep, at least I think I do, in the backseat, in incredible pain since I'm lying on a shoulder that definitely has something wrong with it. I carefully raise the hand of my opposite arm, and feel a strange bump, a bump that's not supposed to be there on my shoulder and I figure, well, I guess that's why it hurts so much.

This time, there is no sighting of Mother, her yellow sweater, my hot chocolate, or birthday pancakes. There's just a strange darkness and I don't feel well, like I have the flu and my whole body hurts, except it's worse than that, and I know I'm about to throw up. I try not to, since I'm in some-body's car, but the rocking from the drive pushes me over the edge of my nausea, and I strain to lean off the car seat and over the car's floor mats, and start to heave.

All that comes up is a bit of foul-tasting water, which is strange, as if I haven't eaten or something.

Didn't I just have hot chocolate and pancakes?

"Hey, no barfing in my car, bitch!" the man driving yells and I force my eyes open to see the back of his head, which has a large bald spot.

Who is he?

We come to a screeching halt, and I hear another man's voice talking about getting me out without getting vomit on himself. I didn't realize there's someone else in the car besides the driver and me.

The car door opens on the side where my feet are, and someone roughly yanks me until I fall into a crumpled ball next to the car. I try to push myself up with my good arm, the one that doesn't have the bumpy shoulder, but pain washes over me, causing me to heave again as if I had something in my stomach.

"Put her over there," one of the men says, and I am dragged over some sort of rough surface, the flesh of my feet being nicked by little rocks and pebbles. It's agonizing, but no worse than the way the rest of my body feels.

When I'm no longer moving, I close my eyes and I'm sleeping again, all my pain gone, and I'm looking for my mother and my birthday presents and my hairbrush.

CHAPTER FORTY-SIX

Niko

I've never cared much about money. Probably because I've always had it. When your father's an established criminal, you're usually pretty well off. I mean, if you're not, that means your dad's a lousy criminal, and men like that don't say in business long, nor do they stay alive.

So if you make it, that means you end up with a fuck load of money. That's why people get into crime to begin with. The promise of riches.

Some people in my world don't like calling what we do criminal. They say they are filling a need. But a pig in lipstick is still a pig.

Is growing up with money nice? I can't really say because I've never *not* had it. The private planes are cool, as are the villas we always vacationed in. I enjoyed them. I got a nice car when I turned fifteen, even though I wasn't old enough to drive it yet, and my brothers and I went to a nice Catholic school until we got kicked out for Kir's fighting. Or was it Vadik's. I don't remember, I was just a little kid.

So we were sent off to another nice, private school, a place that was better equipped to handle boys like my brothers. The thing is, schools like that are the last resort for wealthy families whose kids have been kicked out of other places. These are full of boys like Vadik and Kir, and are basically training grounds for thugs. Wealthy thugs, but thugs, none-theless. It never bothered me though, because I knew from almost the first steps I took, I'd be absorbed into my father's world over time.

I was never on track to become a doctor or lawyer, let's put it that way.

So, men like Charleigh's father, Gil Gates, puzzle me. To an extent. He got himself into a bottomless pit of trouble, one he could never hope to climb out from, and kept digging himself deeper. Each hand he played at our card games carried the hope that he'd not only remedy his problems, his drowning in a sea of debt, but also that he'd shoot into the stratosphere of wealth he so desperately wanted.

If I didn't have money, but wanted it so badly I'd offer my daughter to criminals, would I keep gambling until the hole I was in got deeper and deeper?

I can't say. I am not Gil Gates.

While I have revulsion for the way the man has conducted himself, I also feel pity for him. He's never going to have the life he wants so badly and by reaching so desperately for it, he ended up pushing it even further out of reach.

And then there's Charleigh, who cares little about that sort of thing. We've surrounded her with a level of luxury she probably never even dreamed of, and yet she'd leave it all in a moment.

Which means she'd leave *us*. I'm not going to lie, that hurts.

I want what's best for her. I'm not that selfish that I refuse to see what she wants. If that means a life away from my brothers—away from *me*—then that's what she should have. Although the longer she is involved with us, the less likely it is she'll go back to her former 'civilian' world. Most likely, she will need security protection for the rest of her life. She can really only get that from us guys.

Although all that might be off the table now. My brothers may not agree, but I'm convinced she's in trouble. Frank is dead and she's not answering her phone. She's not out fucking grocery shopping, for Christ's sake. Something has happened to her.

Someone has taken her. The honest truth is, we may never see her again.

We've been looking for her, of course. Our first stop was to have our men stake out Dimitri's place. We came up with nothing. Of course, if that fucker is behind her going missing—to be honest, who else could it be?—she could be anywhere.

On the other hand, there is no end to the people who wish us ill. It's part of our business, part of our way of life. They may not be out and out enemies, per se, but they are definitely men who would love to take us down a notch. Grab some of the power we have. Snake into our business dealings. If they figure Charleigh's important to us—not hard to do since we never put her back up for auction—they'll know we want her for ourselves. And anything we want can be seen as a weakness, ripe for exploitation.

Vadik, on the other hand, is saying she's taken off again, jumping at the first chance she got, either by killing Frank, or having someone else do it. Charleigh might have kicked off her journey there, according to Vadik, because she could snatch her little sister to take her with. If that's true, that Charleigh and her sister are gone, then that leaves only their father available to us. We could always threaten him harm, as we've done before, to get the girls to come out of the woodwork, but at this point

I don't think they are as interested in their father's welfare as they once were.

Kir, who took a big risk in getting attached to Charleigh, is probably worse off than any of us. He'd never admit it, but I know because he's my brother. In fact, he's said barely a word about Charleigh, and even less since she went missing, I think to convince himself she's of no import to him. If he doesn't mention her, doesn't think about her, then she doesn't exist. And if she doesn't exist, he can't get hurt. Again.

It's been years since he lost Clara, and while he's certainly fucked around with the women who throw themselves at him, he's stayed about as far away from caring for anyone as possible. That was beginning to change for him, but now Charleigh's gone.

"Niko. *Niko*," Dominika calls from the office doorway.

My attention snaps to her and for once she isn't wearing a smug smile. She actually has an air about her that's a little uncertain. I know there's not much that can throw this woman off balance. Something is up.

"Yes, Dominika?"

"There's... there's some sort of commotion out front. The doorman just buzzed me."

I flick my computer monitor on, the one that

provides the feeds from our security cameras, and indeed see something happening just outside the club's front door. I enlarge the view, because at first it looks like a homeless person sleeping in our doorway, our bouncer hovering over them, trying to get them to move. But when my view gets closer, I see who it really is.

Holy fucking shit.

CHAPTER FORTY-SEVEN

"Charleigh!" I shout.

I shove aside the bouncer and pull a barely-recognizable Charleigh into my arms. She shrieks with pain and eventually just moans, out of it and unsure what's going on or where she is.

"It's me, baby. It's me, Niko. You're safe now."

"Call my brothers," I yell at the bouncer.

But Dominika already alerted them, and they come flying out the door moments later.

Vadik stops short. "What the fuck?"

Kir hangs back like he's not sure who he's looking at, and as it dawns on him I'm holding Charleigh, he snaps into action.

"C'mon, Niko. Put her in my car. Take her to the compound. She'll be safer there."

He helps me lower Charleigh into his back seat and tosses me the keys. "The little sister's not with her."

I start the car. "You two, go back to the arcade. See if she's there."

They run for Vadik's car and I kick up the gravel in our shitty parking lot, that's how hard I hit the gas as I peel out.

"Charleigh, baby," I say from the front seat, "can you speak, honey? Can you tell me what happened?"

"Wha… what happened," she mumbles.

"Charleigh, listen to me. I need to know who did this to you."

"Who… who did this to me," she mumbles again, her voice weak and pitiful.

Fuck. She's totally out of it.

Once home, I rush her up the stairs of the main house to her room, hollering over my shoulder for the household staff to call our family doctor, and to bring me any bags of frozen vegetables there might in the freezer.

A minute later, the head housekeeper tentatively comes in, peering over my shoulder at Charleigh, where I am doing my best to assess her injuries.

"My God," she gasps with a sob. "Is that… is that Miss Gates?"

I nod. I'm afraid if I start to speak, I might emit a

sob too. I'm okay with doing that in private but not in front of staff. Or anyone, for that matter.

Taking my handkerchief, I wrap a bag of frozen peas and lightly press it to the most swollen side of her face, where her eye is shut, and the bruises are getting deep purple. With my free hand, I push her hair back from her face and she moans again.

Her good eye opens, but she's clearly not focusing on anything. In fact, a slight smile spreads across her face. "It's… it's my birthday," she says quietly. "Mother made me pancakes."

Jesus. What the hell happened to her?

I am to blame. I know I am. I could have done more. I could have listened more. She wouldn't have taken it on herself to find her sister.

And I hate myself for it.

The doctor arrives and asks me to leave the room. I hate to do it, but I agree, if that's how he works. I head to the library for a drink, the stronger the better, when the door flies open with Kir and Vadik rushing in, bringing with them a very unhappy Evie.

Who has some bruises of her own.

They are nothing like her sister's, but I have to assume they were caused by the same people.

Evie is crying, I'm not sure if out of fear of getting in trouble, or because she's in pain, or because she's afraid. I call the housekeeper, who takes her to the kitchen to clean up and get something to eat.

"The doctor is with Charleigh right now," I tell my brothers.

I take a big swig of scotch, hoping it will soothe some of my discomfort, but I can tell it will take a few glasses to relax. In fact, I can't even chill out enough to sit.

"Do we know anything?" Kir asks.

I shake my head as I pace. "No. But I can tell you one thing."

My brothers look at me.

"I love her. And I plan to tell her as soon as she wakes up. If she ever wakes up." My voice cracks.

Shit.

No surprise registers on my brothers' face. There are no attempts to dissuade me from my commitment. No arguments. No discussion.

They understand.

They feel the same way.

CHAPTER FORTY-EIGHT

Niko

When I've waited what I think is long enough for the doctor to do his evaluation, I head back to Charleigh's room taking two steps at a time. I don't want her to be alone, whether with the doctor or anyone else, when she wakes up.

She's quiet now, no more moaning or hallucinating about her mother. As battered as she is, she's relaxed and sleeping, thanks to something I'm sure the doctor gave her.

"How's it going?" I ask him.

He takes a deep breath. "She's badly beaten, as you can see. She has a broken collarbone, which will probably need surgery. But I want to wait a day or so for that. In the meantime, we'll immobilize her arm. But Niko, what's most concerning is this."

I step closer as he lifts Charleigh's filthy shirt. At first it looks like her stomach is covered in dried blood. But when I get closer I see there are actual cuts on her abdomen, like someone carved her skin with a sharp object.

"Holy fuck," I say.

"Yeah," the doctor says quietly.

In jagged, horrific scrawling, the message on her stomach says *apology accepted.*

I freeze, unable to move or speak or even really think. The scotch I've been drinking turns sour in my stomach and I realize I might get sick. I close my eyes and swallow to ward off the nausea when I hear my brothers enter the room behind me.

"How're we doing?" Kir asks.

I turn in their direction but say nothing. I have no words. And when they see Charleigh, they are equally destroyed.

Only the doctor seems capable of speaking. "Do you gentlemen know who might have done this to her?"

I nod quietly. The doctor's been with my family for a long time and knows not to ask too many questions.

He also knows the hospital is the last place we want Charleigh right now, unless of course, it's a matter of life and death.

Hospitals ask questions. We don't want questions.

"Does that say *apology accepted*?" Vadik asks, his face ashen white.

"I'm going to stay with her a little longer, make sure she's stable," the doctor says.

I gulp. I have to ask the question I know everyone in the room is thinking. "Doctor, can you tell… I mean… was she…?"

I can't even say the goddamn words.

"It appears not. If she had been… assaulted, I would be insisting we go to the hospital right now for an exam. But whoever did this to her, it was obviously to send a message. Nothing sexual in nature about it."

Oh thank God. Thank fucking God.

"Doctor, can you excuse my brothers and me for a few minutes? Maybe you could head down to the kitchen for coffee or something," Vadik suggests.

With a nod, the doctor excuses himself and pulls the bedroom door shut quietly behind him.

Kir starts pacing the room, running his fingers through his hair. I only know this because I can see him from the corner of my eye. It's Charleigh's battered face I can't take my eyes off of. Even with swelling and bruising, I can still see her quiet beauty.

"This is the work of Dimitri. The *Pakhan* told us

to apologize to him, which is what the message must be in reference to. But he wasn't in the meeting," Kir says. "So, how did he know?"

I look at my brothers and know we're thinking the same thing. After all, it's not hard to figure out. But I want to kick myself for not anticipating this. I almost always know what's coming. But I missed the signs for this one, big time.

Vadik sits on the edge of the bed and takes one of Charleigh's hands, surprising both himself and me. "Yes. The *Pakhan's* second in command, that lousy fucker. *He* told Dimitri. He's been in that guy's pocket all along."

Fucking number two guy. He could be killed for repeating what went on in a meeting with the *Pakhan*.

"That's why he was advocating so hard for Dimitri. He's his friend but must also be on his payroll."

Bastard.

"I'm going to see the *Pakhan*," Vadik says, heading for the door.

But Kir stops him by literally stepping in front of him. "Wait, Vadik. Hold on. Let's think this through."

He's right. Nothing is gained by acting without thinking.

My brothers chat on the other side of the room.

This gives me a moment with Charleigh. I bend to whisper in her ear. "Baby, I don't know if you can hear me. But I'm not leaving you. I'll stay with you until you are better. Because I love you."

CHAPTER FORTY-NINE

Kir

"You look like an angry guard dog."

Niko frowns at me. "Fuck off, asshole."

My brother lifts himself from the easy chair where he slept, right next to Charleigh's bed, and winces from having spent the night in an awkward position. He's still wearing his dress clothes from the day before.

"Dude you could have at least put on some sweats and a T-shirt. You would have been a lot more comfortable."

He looks at Charleigh, whose forehead I'm checking for fever. "What's going on?" he asks.

"I called the doctor about an hour ago to give him an update. She should be waking up soon. Hopefully she'll be able to tell us what happened," I say.

At that moment, Vadik joins us with Evie on his heels like a nervous little puppy. Her eyes and nose are red, as if she cried all night.

When she sees Charleigh, she sobs loudly and runs across the room, throwing her arms around her. "Char, please be okay. I'm sorry. I'm so sorry," she sobs.

"Careful, Evie," I say, pulling her off her sister. "She has a broken clavicle."

At this news, Evie breaks into howling sobs. If Charleigh is on the verge of waking, she certainly will now.

The kid feels like shit. And she should.

"Does she know what went down?" Niko asks.

Vadik and I nod. Earlier this morning, when Evie was crying in the room we made up for her, Vadik and I went in to see what was up. I don't know if it was out of guilt or sisterly love, but she spilled the whole story. Or as much of it as she knew.

She admitted she'd lured Charleigh to the arcade but swore she didn't know it was so anyone could hurt her. She thought all the boys just wanted to meet her beautiful older sister, and wanting to be part of the crowd, she had no issue with going along.

But Dimitri showed up and Evie protested in her sister's defense, it became clear that Arseny had just used her to lure Charleigh, so Dimitri could pounce on her. When she tried to chase after the men who made off with her sister, she was smacked around until she agreed to shut her mouth.

Niko shakes his head sadly and turns to take a look at Evie, who's still sobbing over her sister, clutching Charleigh's hand to her heart like her own is breaking.

It's sad to see the kid so shook up, but hell, if this doesn't teach her a lesson about getting her shit together, nothing will.

I have to admit, I have no idea how to soothe a sobbing teenage girl. None of us do. So we just let her cry it out, occasionally checking back over our shoulders to see if Charleigh's woken yet.

This is Niko's worse nightmare come true. All along he was convinced something had happened to Charleigh. He was right, except maybe he hadn't expected her to be quite so bad off.

Myself, I was on the fence. I could have gone in either direction with my theories about where she'd gone. She could have taken off just as well as been taken. I didn't have a strong feeling either way.

But Vadik, he's the one who was convinced she ran again. He was pissed about it too. And I can tell he feels like shit right now. He said she ran once, why wouldn't she try it again? A reasonable assumption in his mind. But he called it wrong and when she finds out what he was thinking, I wonder if she'll forgive him.

Next time I turn around, I see Evie has climbed up onto Charleigh's bed and is snuggling as close to her as she can get without lying right on her. She's clasping the hand from Charleigh's good arm, and her eyes are already closed.

Two sleeping beauties.

After Dimitri took off with Charleigh, Evie was roughed up and told to keep her mouth shut by Arseny. She made herself small and hid in a dark corner of the arcade, hoping to escape unnoticed. Vadik and I arrived not knowing what we'd find. But she must have recognized my voice from the time I met her at her school. She bounded out of hiding and hardly let go of us until we arrived back at the compound.

The head housekeeper took her to get cleaned up and put her to bed. We'd intended to keep her from seeing Charleigh in her current condition, but that plan was shot to hell. Maybe it's just as well, though. Teach the kid a lesson. Maybe this will keep her on the straight and narrow, at least for a while.

My brothers keep talking but I turn back to Charleigh. There she lies with her sister, more like mother and daughter than sister and sister.

Charleigh took on a lot when her mother died. Life has not given her much of a break.

Everyone gets a shitty hand now and then but some people get more than one. It's not fucking fair.

This isn't good, these feelings I have for Charleigh. My skin crawls with the urge to run away before my heart gets stomped on like it was by Clara's death. A big piece of me went with her after that car accident, and if something like that happens again, I'm pretty sure I won't survive.

It's an ugly fact.

Since Evie is holding Charleigh's one good hand, I lay mine on top of both sisters', feeling both their warmth and also their vulnerability. It's kind of the two of them against the world. Their mother's death left them dangling in the wind because it also took a big part of their father when it happened.

"Come on, baby," I whisper to Charleigh. "You can do this."

At the sound of my voice, she moans lightly in her sleep. Evie's eyes pop open. "Is she awake?" she asks hopefully.

"Not yet." I get up to leave. I have business to take care of. We all do. "Evie, I'm going to ask one thing of you, and it's that you stay by your sister's side all day. Do not leave her unless you have to go to the bathroom. I do not want her waking up alone."

Evie begins to throw me her snarky teenage face, so I pull my suit jacket open a little, just enough for her to see my gun holster, which I pat. "Don't fuck with me, Evie. I'm not as nice as your high school principal."

Her mouth drops open and her eyes are wide, and I think maybe I made some progress and at the end of all this, we might see a new Evie.

CHAPTER FIFTY

CHARLEIGH

"Are you sure this is the right thing to do, Miss?"

The housekeeper guides me down the stairs, although I insisted several times I can make it on my own. It's been a few days since my 'accident,' as she calls it, and she has gently let it be known, multiple times, that I need to take it easy. Or at least easier than I have been.

It feels good to be mothered. I've forgotten what it was like.

My broken clavicle has been set and I'm wearing my arm in a sling on that side of my body, something about keeping weight off it. The swelling on my face is nearly gone, although I still have colorful bruises and black eyes. It's kind of amazing, how fast the face heals.

Getting by with one arm is not nearly as hard as I thought it would be. I didn't put on any makeup before leaving the house today, though. Not so much because it's tricky with one arm—it's that I want people to *see* my bruises. I want them to see what Dimitri and his men did to me. And that I survived.

I also want everyone to know what happens to Dimitri when the Alekseev brothers catch up to him, which they will. No doubt he knows there's a price on his head now for what he did to me, and that he's deep in hiding. But he'll eventually slip up, and before he closes his eyes for the last time, the guys will make my injuries look minor compared to what they give him.

A few short weeks ago, I never would have wished this on anyone, even someone who hurt me as badly as Dimitri did. But I'm different now. I can't say that's better or worse—I haven't decided. But someone can only take so much in this life and not turn into something different. I'm not proud of it, but I also didn't ask for it, this shit show. It was bound to change me. And it has.

I tried to hang onto my humanity, I really did.

My stomach is still crisscrossed with bandages where they carved a message into my skin. Lucky for me, they didn't cut deeply enough for stitches, although I will probably end up with scars. Vadik and his brothers promise to cover any procedure I want to correct it, but I might just keep them as a reminder of what I endured.

"I'll be okay, thank you," I say when I reach the front door.

I pull Niko's keys out of my pocket. "I'm heading straight to the club. The doctor says I'm fine to drive."

"One handed?" she asks.

"Yeah. It will be fine," I say.

I click the alarm button on Niko's car and the doors unlock. Where Frank was murdered. That hurts more than any of my injuries, to be honest.

Poor Frank, who was just accommodating my obsessive drive to protect my sister. He never thought we were walking into the kind of ambush we did, and for the first time in his bodyguard career, he was caught completely unaware.

It was a fatal mistake. One I blame myself for.

I don't know what they did with his body nor how they cleaned the car of his blood and brains. All that was taken care of during the couple days I was in and out of consciousness. When I asked, I was told point blank that the Alekseevs have people to handle things like this. That was the end of that conversation.

My dear, dear Frank.

I remember passing by him when Dimitri walked me out of the arcade. For a second, he looked like he'd just nodded off to sleep. His face was so peaceful. His huge hands still held his phone, where a news cast was playing. But he was angled awkwardly, and the blood on his temple told the full story.

It breaks my heart. The guys don't know if he has any family or not. He never talked to me about personal things. But we'll find out if there is anyone out there, and ensure they are compensated for the loss.

Just as I'm about to take off, Evie bounds out of the house, her hair still wet from the shower. She looks so fresh without her usual black-ringed eyes and pale foundation. Not like a girl who's lived through some of the things she has.

"Hey, where are you going?" she asks, catching up to me breathlessly.

"To the club for a bit. You stay here with the housekeeper, please."

Evie rolls her eyes. "Oh, come on. Let me come with you. I want to see where the guys work."

I look over her shoulder and nod at the house-keeper, who smiles, waves, and heads back into the house.

I am sure this woman, when she went to work for the Alekseev family, never expected babysitting duty. But if it bothers her, she doesn't let on.

"All right," I say, sighing.

I really don't want Evie hanging out at the club, but it might be better for me to keep an eye on her for the time being. The guys are looking for Dimitri and his men, but finding them might take some time. Until then, they've stressed we must all be very careful. Just because Dimitri struck again, the first time being his murder of the brothers' parents, doesn't mean he's done with his attacks.

As Evie climbs into the car, I do a quick sweep of in the interior to make sure there isn't any evidence missed by the cleaners. The last thing I need is for her to know what went on here.

It feels good to drive again, and I know Evie and I are safe because security insisted on driving behind us on the short drive to the club. I'm actually surprised they let me drive at all, having been instructed by the guys to keep a close watch on my sister and me. But I think they also know when to pick their battles, and if I want to go for a drive, to work with me to make it happen.

Everybody wins that way.

When we get to the club, I walk with my shoulders back and chin up. My injuries are more than evident, and I'm not going to pretend I want to hide them, because I don't. I'm not ashamed or embarrassed. I've done nothing wrong.

Evie is less than impressed with the club, and she doesn't bother to hide her disdain for the building exterior or its surroundings. "*This* is where they work? Don't they have enough money to move someplace nicer?" she asks, turning up her nose.

"C'mon," I say impatiently, catching her hand and pulling her behind me. "It's nicer inside. You'll see."

We head up to the top floor via the usual elevator, Evie looking around the whole time with wide eyes. A week ago, if I'd brought her here, she'd have been in her teenage goth stage. But now she looks like a regular, freckle-faced sixteen-year-old.

How fast things change. A week ago, I would have done anything to keep Evie away from this place. Now, she is going to learn about the Alekseev's world. And she's going to learn about it very quickly.

"Oh my God, Charleigh!"

Stacey throws her arms around me the moment we enter the dressing room and I'm so happy to see her, I want to cry. "You're here," she shrieks. "I'm so happy to see you."

She holds me at arms' length, taking in my

injuries. Her eyes fill with tears but she sniffles and forces a smile.

She looks wonderful, all traces of Alexei's brutal treatment having faded. At least on the outside, that is.

"When did you get back here, back to work?" I ask.

Evie's looking between the two of us, wondering what we're talking about. Hopefully I can get away with not telling her. Ever.

"I returned day before yesterday. I was so freaked when I heard what happened. Who do you think—"

But I cut her off. We didn't need to have this discussion in front of Evie.

"Hey, this is my kid sister, Evie."

"Oh my God, you two look so much alike," she squeals, zeroing in on the bruise on Evie's cheek.

My cutting her off worked. She got the message to table any sharing of details until later.

"Nice to meet you," Evie says, extending her hand.

My God. I didn't know she had it in her.

"The Gates girls," she laughs. "Sounds like a TV show. So, what are you guys doing here?"

I glance around the dumpy dressing room, and wonder if Dominika is still stashing her photos here.

"I'm just popping by. Evie will wait here in the dressing room. Right Evie?"

I give her my best stink eye, my warning not to pull any crap. I don't have it in me to deal with any of her teen drama today. Not sure I ever will, again.

Stacey glances at her vibrating phone. "Ugh. My kid is sick and I have to pick him up from school and bring him to my mother's."

"Do you have anyone to cover for you?" I ask.

I know that her son's school and her mother are not far.

"Yeah, I suppose. But… my car is in the shop. It's always something, isn't it?" she says with a hopeless laugh.

It surely is.

She picks up her phone and starts tapping. "I'll just call an Uber. I was trying to save money, but between a broken-down car and having to pay for rides, I'll just take on extra shifts." She sighs.

But I have an idea. "Hey, take Niko's car. I'm sure it's fine."

I offer her the keys.

She screws up her face. "Really? No, I'd better not." Shaking her head, she waves away my suggestion.

"Hey. I'm absolutely sure. Go ahead. Just come right back."

She frowns, but she's considering it. I can tell. "You are a godsend," she says, giving me a big kiss on the cheek. "But I don't think I should. Doesn't he drive a fancy car?"

I laugh. "Yeah it's fancy, at least if you ask me. Which is why you should take it. Seriously. He'll be okay with it."

"Okay. I'll be right back." She grabs the keys, her purse, and heads for the door.

"Hey, can I go with her?" Evie asks. "I don't want to hang out in this creepy place."

I take a step closer to my sister. "No, you may not. Stay here with me, where you're safe."

And the old Evie is back, rolling her eyes and sneering at me.

"I don't mind if she comes. We can get to know each other," Stacey says.

"Thanks, but not today. There are some… issues the guys need to resolve. Until they are, Evie stays close to me. And I stay close to the guys. Now go get your boy before Dominika sees you're missing."

Stacey grins one last time, and dashes out the door.

"What are these costumes?" Evie asks, picking through the stripper garb on the hanging rack.

"I'll tell you another time. I need to talk to the guys. Wait here for me, okay?"

"But I don't want to—"

I close the dressing room door in the face of Evie's complaining, wishing I could lock her in there. Although she might protest, I don't think she'll be leaving my side for a long time, given recent events.

CHAPTER FIFTY-ONE

CHARLEIGH

I join the brothers in Niko's office.

He welcomes me with a soft hand on my back and I unintentionally flinch. I don't mean to. It's just that things are… different now.

"I have a request of you all," I say.

Vadik's eyebrows shoot up. "You do? What is it?"

He looks amused by my serious tone.

"I know you're planning to go to war. I heard that your people know where Dimitri is now."

Vadik looks at his brothers with a slight grin. "Damn. Our girl here is learning the biz." He laughs lightly.

Kir and Niko don't join him.

"We are, Charleigh. Why do you bring it up? You

don't need to know any details about our... work. It's better for you this way."

"I'm asking you to wait. I want to be part of your team. You have to let me take care of this myself."

All three of the guys' eyebrows rise this time, and I have to say I think I've rendered them speechless.

For once.

"I deserve this. You owe it to me. Let things simmer for a while until I am stronger. Let Dimitri come out of hiding thinking everything is going to be fine. That he got the last word and taught you guys a lesson."

I'm shaking while I say this, because although I practiced my little speech in the bathroom mirror, the odds of the guys complying with my request are slim. Very slim.

But I figure it's worth a shot. I'm here because of them. This is the very least they can give me.

And the more I think about it, the more I burn with rage. I will make Dimitri suffer like he made me. I will humiliate him and make him cry.

Just like he did to me.

The brothers look at me with concern, like I've gone off my rocker or something. Hell, maybe I have.

It doesn't matter.

They know how I feel because they've been where I am right now.

"You've wanted to take out Dimitri for two years. Surely waiting a few more days, a week at most, won't hurt," I add, putting on my best badass face.

Which is probably not saying much.

Kir speaks first. "I… I think that's a reasonable request. What about you guys?" he asks.

Niko nods slowly. "I'm good with it. But Charleigh, it takes time to learn what we do. You don't become an expert marksman overnight."

Holy shit. They're considering my request. I'm actually swaying them.

"I know, Niko. But you have to let me be part of the team in some capacity. Please. You know I never ask for anything."

They can't argue with that.

"I'll tell you what, Charleigh," Vadik says, "we'll let it rest for now. We'll get you set up with the shooting range. One of our security guys can take you there. But no promises about who takes out Dimitri. That's to be decided among my brothers and me."

I want to jump up and down, but there's really nothing happy about wanting to kill a man. What the hell is wrong with me?

I may not have gotten everything I asked for, but this is a huge concession.

"Thank you," I say, "thank you so much."

"So, take a seat, won't you?" Vadik offers, pointing toward a chair.

I settle in and I have to admit, I'm a little tickled by the surprise that each of the guys wears on his face. It's so satisfying that not everything about me is so damn predictable.

"Our girl has some serious claws," Vadik says, studying me. "What I wonder is, if she always had these claws or if she's just developed them since she's been with us."

I know what Vadik is asking. The same question his brothers are thinking too, most likely.

How different am I? How much have I changed? Is there anything about me that resembles the girl I was before Dimitri hurt me?

Will they ever see the old Charleigh again? The one they care so much about?

And even if they were to ask me these questions out loud, I wouldn't answer them. I couldn't, not even if I wanted to.

Because I don't have the answers. Is my thirst for revenge a phase? Something that will fade in time?

Or am I permanently changed?

"Time will tell," I say simply, and they know

exactly what I mean. Nothing more has to be said on the subject.

They will or won't include me. I can't do anything further about it, aside from asking.

"You know, Charleigh, there is something my brothers and I have wanted to discuss with you. It's been on our minds for a while, but we only decided to bring it up with you, given recent events," Vadik says.

If I'm not mistaken, Niko looks a teeny bit nervous, and Kir is looking out the window, avoiding my gaze.

Jesus, men are predictable.

"Okay. What's up—" I start to ask.

But the office door flies open and Dominika bursts in. She doesn't look well.

Displeased, Vadik clicks his tongue. "Dominika, I've asked you to knock before coming in, you know—"

Vadik's scolding is ignored and she swallows hard. "Sorry but… I… this is an emergency. I just got a call… There's been an accident."

I sit up straight in my seat. An accident? Who got in an accident?

Her mouth opens and closes, but nothing comes out.

"What, Dominika? Out with it," Kir snaps.

Squeezing her eyes shut, she swallows to regain her composure. "I got a call from the police that four blocks from here, Niko's car blew up. Stacey was in it."

I shriek as my hand flies to my mouth.

"I didn't believe it," she says, her voice shaking, "so I drove over. It was horrible…" she says, grasping the doorway for balance, covering her mouth with her other hand as if she might get sick.

Niko jumps to his feet. "What? What would Stacey be doing in my car?" he asks, looking at me.

The room spins and when I can finally speak, my voice breaks. "I… I gave her the keys. I loaned her the car to pick up her sick kid at school. She said she'd be right back. It was supposed to be a quick errand." I double over right in my seat, gasping for air while tears start down my face. The pain is greater than my recent beating, if that's possible.

Not Stacey, no. Her son… and her mother.

Is this another death that's all my fault? How will I live with myself?

Niko runs to his desk, and all three guys start making phone calls, I don't know why or to whom. I don't have the capacity to think.

That's when an icy realization washes over me and I'm pretty certain I will lose my breakfast in the next few seconds.

"WAIT," I try to shout. But it comes out as more of a broken squeak.

Fortunately, I am heard, and everyone looks my way.

I slowly turn to Dominika. "Where is my sister? I left her in the dressing room."

The guys stop what they are doing and the air in the room gets rancid and strange colors dance before my eyes. I'm freezing and yet I can feel myself sweating.

Please God, please God, please God.

Please *Mother*. Help me. Help me now, if you have ever been able to. I need you.

Dominika looks at me like I'm crazy. "I saw a girl in the hallway earlier, a teenager, running for the elevator. I wasn't able to ask her what she was doing because I was talking to a club member. That was your sister? I can tell you she's not in the dressing room. I was just in there to get my purse. I think she left."

I push past Dominika and run. I have to find my sister.

I can't lose anybody else.

Evie.

Find out what happens to Charleigh in the next
Beauty & the Bratva novel,
Vicious Revenge

Dear Reader:

I'm USA TODAY bestselling romance author Mika Lane, and am OBSESSED with bringing you sassy, steamy stories with imperfect heroines and the bad-a*s dudes they bring to their knees. I'll always bring you my signature humor and heat, topped off with a modern-day happily ever after.

My first book ever was *The Day I Ate the Milkyway,* a true fourth-grade masterpiece illustrated with crayons and bound with construction paper and glue. Nowadays, steamy romance gives purpose to my days and nights as I create worlds and characters that tickle the imagination. I live in magical Northern California with my own handsome alpha dude, sometimes known as Mr. Mika Lane, and two devilish cats named Chuck and Murray.

A dual citizen of the United States and Ireland, I have on more than one occasion spent my last dollar on a plane ticket somewhere, and am always planning my next escape. I often try new recipes on unsuspecting friends, search out hiding places to read undisturbed, and sadly kill every houseplant I bring home.

I LOVE to hear from readers when I'm not dreaming up naughty tales to share. Visit my online shop https://mikalaneshop.com/ and say hello https://mikalaneshop.com/pages/meet-mika.

xoxo, Mika